Prescription for Admission

To my family, who inspire, support, and believe.

Monique S. Nugent MD, MPH

Prescription for Admission

A Doctor's Guide for Navigating the Hospital, Advocating for Yourself, and Having a Better Hospitalization

Copyright © 2023 Monique Nugent

All rights reserved. No part of this publication may be reproduced, distributed, or transmitted in any form or by any means, including photocopying, recording, or other electronic or mechanical methods, without the prior written permission of the publisher, except in the case of brief quotations embodied in critical reviews and certain other noncommercial uses permitted by copyright law. For permission requests, write to the publisher, addressed "Attention: Permissions Coordinator," at the address below.

P.O. Box 747
Norwell, MA 02061

ISBN: 979-8-9869301-1-4 (paperback)
ISBN: 979-8-9869301-0-7 (ebook)

Ordering Information:
Special discounts are available on quantity purchases by corporations, associations, and others. For details, visit https://drmoniquenugent.com/.

Table of Contents

Download Your Quick Guide to the Hospital 7

Letter to the Reader i

How to Use This Book v

Part One: Pre-Day One 1
    Prepare for Your Hospitalization 3
    Basic Medical Information You Should Know.................... 5
    Specialized Care Providers.. 13
    What to Bring to the Hospital 18
    What Are the Different Types of Hospitals? 22

Part Two: In the Emergency Department 27
    But First, a Few Technicalities.. 29
    Your First Conversation in the ED 36
    Medication Reconciliation 40
    Should I Stay, or Should I Go?... 44
    A Fork in the Road 47

Part Three: Day One 49
    Admission and Stabilization... 51
    Big Goals and Little Goals 54
    Code Status and Advance Directive 59
    Planning Ahead: Advance Directives and Healthcare
        Proxy.. 71
    Diet 76

Part Four: Day Two 87
    Fact-Finding and Plan-Making 89

    Clinical Testing 90
    Social Issues 105
    Healthcare Inequity 112
    Tips from Your Hospitalist 117

Part Five: Days Three and Four 125
    Treatment 127
    Family Meetings 143

Part Six: Day Five 151
    Leaving the Hospital 153
    Post–Acute Care Facilities 154
    Transfer to Another Acute Hospital 159
    End-of-Life Care After Discharge: Hospice 163
    Getting Ready to Leave 172
    "Home" May Look Different 178
    The Logistics of Leaving 180
    Welcome Home 184

After Discharge 189

Goodbye for Now 191

Download Your Quick Guide to the Hospital

Please use this QR code to download a quick guide of this book, which includes condensed information and fillable sections. You can save the PDF to your phone or print it and fill it out so that you will have it in the event you or a loved one is hospitalized.

Letter to the Reader

Dear reader,

I once overheard two patients talking in their shared room about various frustrations with their experiences in the hospital. One patient openly expressed that she felt overwhelmed, saying, "I just don't know who to talk to or what to do. It's like I'm just getting pulled along, and I don't know where I'm going to end up."

Her roommate, who was trying to be supportive, suggested that she speak to a more senior physician. "Have you asked to talk to the chief resident? On *Grey's Anatomy*, they always get the chief resident to put everyone in line." Being chief resident at the time, I couldn't help but be flattered by her assumptions of my power, but as her physician, my heart broke to hear that a TV drama was her reference for how to navigate her hospital stay.

Often when patients interact with the behemoth that is U.S. healthcare, they find it too confusing, too opaque, and too cumbersome for them to feel fully in control. The most overwhelming of all places for patients tends to be the hospital. Coming to the hospital means that you are already sick, in pain, and unable to do much on your own. Patients can feel like things move at warp speed in the hospital and feel as if they're meeting 10 people an hour who are demanding 20 different things and giving 30 different opinions.

And when it finally comes time for discharge, even though people want to get back home, they often feel as if they have many more questions than answers in addition to a bunch of new medications and doctor appointments. Managing all of these adjustments at home can be just as overwhelming as the hospital stay itself. The whole thing can feel like a carnival ride.

I've built my career around hospitals. I'm a hospitalist (an internist who specializes in caring for acutely hospitalized people), and hospitals are kind of my comfort zone. I love the pace of a hospital, the teamwork between doctors and nurses, and the bonds I build with specialists. I know that amazing things can happen in hospitals and have seen people's lives saved by astute clinicians over and over again. But I've also seen how easily patients and their families can get lost in the same place I'm most comfortable—a place that is meant to care for and support them.

When I decided to write this book, I did so with all the overwhelmed patients I've met over the years in mind.

This book is meant to be a sort of traveler's guide to your acute hospitalization, in addition to furnishing you with lists of critical information you should know about yourself, things to pack, and questions to ask. This book will give you tips on what to do when you're feeling stuck—and will also help you learn how to not get stuck in the first place.

What you will not find in this book are treatment plans or diagnostic ramblings, as your individual care is best left to the clinicians who are seeing you in person. Rather, I want you to read this book and come away with *your* game plan for each day in the hospital, *your* list of needs and questions, and *your* mechanisms for communicating with the care team and advocating for yourself. Even though you have this book, there may still be times that you feel as if you're being pulled along in the hospital, but I hope that you will be able to flip back through these pages when you're alone and make a game plan to break that pattern.

Being sick is never easy. During my training I had an attending physician say, "Patients are going to get worse until they start getting better. It is our job to make sure they get to the better part." That wisdom has always stuck with me, because I know that when you're sick, the better part seems so far away. For me, I think of every day as a chance to find or redefine what the better part is—because, trust me, you'll make it there.

–Monique S. Nugent MD, MPH

How to Use This Book

You will notice this book is split into several different parts, centered around five "days." This number was chosen because the average length of a hospitalization in the U.S. is around five and a half days.[1] This book will walk you through virtually everything you can expect to happen on each day, as well as what steps you should take to participate in your care.

I've focused on specific topics for each day of hospitalization in this book, in what is typically the chronological order you can expect. However, it is important to note that all of the topics discussed can come up on any day of your hospitalization, so use the table of contents to quickly find something specific.

There are a few sections that will have room for you to fill in some personal information or write down your thoughts. You should use those pages as a template for you to re-create those lists in a place you will have easy access to or, easier still, take a picture with your cell phone.

You will notice a few callout boxes entitled "Real Talk." These are little pearls of extra information that will give a fuller picture to the topics they are embedded in.

Finally, I've asked my close friend, Dr. Nyota Pieh to contribute some high-yield pointers on how to manage your mental health needs during a hospitalization. We've titled her sections "Dr. Pieh's Mental Health Corner." Dr. Pieh is a board-certified psychiatrist and has spent a lot of time working with patients who

---

1 Audrey J. Weiss and Anne Elixhauser, "Overview of Hospital Stays in the United States, 2012," October 2014, https://hcup-us.ahrq.gov/reports/statbriefs/sb180-Hospitalizations-United-States-2012.pdf.

are hospitalized for an acute medical illness and need psychiatric care. She has completed fellowships in public psychiatry, emergency psychiatry, and psychosomatic medicine. I found her writings to be very valuable, and I know you will too.

The point of this book is to furnish you with high-value information so you know how to be an active driver of your care and understand how get the most out of every interaction with the various healthcare professionals you will meet during a hospitalization.

Over the course of my career, I've come to realize that the healthcare system asks patients and loved ones to navigate a system that is very, very complicated—keeping in mind that these patients, probably not unlike yourself, are not medically inclined and may never have interacted with the multiple systems within a hospital.

I consider this book a valuable source of knowledge for anyone faced with a hospitalization, and it can be used at any point during a hospital stay.

My hope is that you do not feel 100% unprepared to be in the hospital. So, even if you feel 98% unprepared after reading the details herein, I know this book will have made a difference because that's 2% more information than you started with, and even that small amount can make a big difference—trust me.

Part One: Pre-Day One

Prepare for Your Hospitalization

In the years that I've been a hospitalist, I've come to recognize that when it comes to how prepared people are for a hospitalization, most patients fall into two categories:
1. Those who have never really needed a hospital and are almost certainly surprised that they will need to stay in the hospital.
2. People who struggle with some chronic or progressive illness and have required a few prior hospitalizations.

Chronic (e.g., congestive heart disease) and/or progressive medical illnesses (e.g., multiple sclerosis) can be difficult to manage, often requiring a team of medical specialists and a network of support services. Even those who do their best to follow their care plan and keep in close contact with their primary care provider (PCP) and specialists may find themselves dealing with very symptomatic flare-ups or even an acute crisis due to their chronic illness. Such sudden issues are why someone may find themselves hospitalized a few times a year, or even a few times over several months, while clarifying a diagnosis or dealing with acute changes.

If you're dealing with a chronic or progressive disease process, my best advice is that you have a pre-hospital checklist. Your pre-hospital checklist will be something you and your loved ones can refer to the next time you are hospitalized, allowing everyone to quickly know what you will need to get you through it. With a pre-hospital checklist, you and your loved ones will be organized and prepared for your hospitalization, rather than feeling out of control by trying to gather resources and information at the last minute.

For those who end up hospitalized due to an accident or a sudden illness, you may ask, "Is a pre-hospital checklist even possible?"

The answer is...yes!

It is important to know some very basic information about yourself, your medical history, and whom you want to be your healthcare proxy. And if you can't keep all that information at the top of your mind by yourself, knowing where such medical specifics are already documented will make any unexpected trip to the hospital easier and safer.

Regardless of whether or not this is your first or 15th hospitalization, there are some key things you should know about yourself that will make your time in the hospital more efficient, effective, and safe—and it should only take you a few minutes to retrieve them!

Basic Medical Information You Should Know

Your medical team's number one job during a hospitalization is to ensure your safety. It just so happens that the best way for them to do that is by having all the correct and pertinent information they need to make sound medical decisions and to create a safe and effective treatment plan.

Information is key, and thus you will be asked numerous questions about your medical history and the situation surrounding your current medical concerns. If you feel uncomfortable giving certain information, such as your sexual history or use of drugs or alcohol, please know that your open and honest answers should be met with compassion and will give your team a better opportunity to make a care plan that suits your needs and keeps you safe.

No matter whether you're a category one or category two patient, here's what you need to know in order to be prepared for the hospital:

1. Current Medications
2. Past Medical and Surgical History
3. Allergies to Medications and Foods
4. Alcohol and Drug Use
5. Bonus Item: Family History

As we move through these items, you can use the worksheet at the end of this section to write down your information, then take a picture of it on your cell phone and save it. If you have a different method that you prefer for storing this information, please use it—what's most important is that you have all of this information saved somewhere accessible.

Current Medications

This is a big one, which is why I'm starting with it first.

If you take any medications—prescribed medications, over-the-counter medicines, herbal supplements or vitamins, your sister's Valium, whatever—you will need to tell your care team what they are. Ideally, you should know the name, the dose, and how often you're taking any medication.

For example, I'd love for you to be able to tell your hospitalist, "I take 25 mg of hydrochlorothiazide every morning at eight for my blood pressure." But honestly, I'm happy if you just know the name and how many times a day you take the medication.

So, take this time to write down all the medications you are currently taking. Head to your medicine cabinet right now and use the example below to write everything down in the template on page 16.

Go. Right now. You've got this.

Medication List

Name	Dose	Frequency
Acetaminophen	1,000 mg	Three times a day when in pain
Metoprolol	50 mg	Two times a day
Loratadine	10 mg	Once a day

The names of prescription medications aren't always accessible or easy to remember, which is why I highly recommend you write down these details now. However, when you're in the hospital, if you can't get access to your medication list, you can tell your physician the name and location of the pharmacy that fills your prescriptions. Many hospitals have software programs that allow them to access retail pharmacy records and see what you've been prescribed, which doctor prescribed it, and when you last filled your prescription. If needed, someone can also call the pharmacy directly to get that information. Furthermore, state health departments (or similar government bodies) often keep records of how often someone is prescribed opiate pain medications and other controlled substances, so your physician will have access to those records as well.

Finally, please be honest about how you're taking your medicines. What you've been prescribed and what you're actually taking can be two completely different things.

If you are taking your medication in a way that is different from how the prescription order is written, please say so. The way you answer questions about medications can affect your physician's ability to make a diagnosis and treatment plan. Misunderstanding how and what medications you are taking or supposed to be taking can even lead to poor outcomes, which we definitely want to avoid.

For instance, let's say you are prescribed 10 units of insulin, but you're only taking five units, or perhaps you're not using the insulin at all; tell your doctor that you are taking a lower dose than prescribed. Otherwise, your physician may think, "Hmm, his blood sugars are really high even though he is taking ten units of insulin. I will increase the dose to twenty units, because he clearly needs more insulin." That may be a high dose of insulin for you that could result in hypoglycemia (low blood sugar) and add a day or so onto your hospitalization while your physician makes a new plan for your diabetes.

Past Medical and Surgical History

I've always joked that my favorite type of patient to do admission with is the one who hands me a folder with a typed list of their medications, chronic medical conditions, surgical procedures, and a copy of their last electrocardiogram (ECG/EKG). (Yes, these people really do exist.) But the truth is, most people visiting the hospital come in under a bit of duress, and they're usually unable to recall some things, especially the finer details of their medical journey, while some are not able to give me more than the most basic information about themselves.

So, what do those extremes mean for you? I want you to be somewhere in between the person with an alphabetized binder and the person who doesn't really know what medical conditions they have, why they take any prescribed medications, or what surgeries they've had in the past. I'd like you to be able to give the highlights of your medical journey, focusing on any chronic medical condition you have and the current status of it. If you know some fine details about your condition, then that's an added bonus, but it's not necessary.

For example, let's say you need to wear oxygen at home for chronic obstructive pulmonary disease (COPD), so you tell your hospitalist, "I wear oxygen all the time because of COPD." That's helpful information to know, period. Now, if you can say, "I use two liters of oxygen all the time, but recently I've needed four liters of oxygen"—*jackpot*! Not only can those specifics help me figure out what caused you to come to the hospital in the first place, but you've also given information that tells me just how sick you really are.

Knowing why you had surgery falls under this category too. I distinctly remember being an intern and seeing a pretty fresh-looking surgical scar on my patient's abdomen, then glancing back at their chart but not being able to find details about any prior surgery.

"Excuse me," I said with my most impressive, "I'm a new doctor, so please take me seriously" poker face, "Why did you recently have a procedure done? Here, on your belly."

The patient paused, scratching his forehead while scanning his memory. "Uh...yeah. You know what—I don't know."

This happens all the time. Many patients have told me that they didn't know what surgery or procedure they had done, or why. And yet, it's important that we know your surgical history because, depending on the surgery, there can be some very specific things we could expect, or your treatment plan may need to be adjusted.

My suggestion? Anytime someone's going to cut you open, please know why, try to remember it, or write it down somewhere that you will be able to access easily. You don't have to know the name of the surgery—I don't expect you to remember the term *cholecystectomy*—but you should be able to say, "I had surgery to remove my gallbladder." (You should also add this info to the worksheet on page 16 where you've been writing your medication information.)

Allergies to Medications and Foods

You will be asked about allergies to medications and foods several times during your hospitalization. Avoiding medications to which you are allergic will help ensure your safety. In addition to knowing the name of the medication to which you have an allergy, it is very helpful to know what type of reaction you have had to said medication and how severe that reaction was. Ideally, I'd like you to be able to say something like this:

"I'm allergic to penicillin. It gives me a really itchy rash. I'm also severely allergic to peanuts and have needed to use an EpiPen in the past."

This statement clearly tells me what medications and foods you should avoid and what the possible consequences are if you are exposed to them.

Misconceptions abound about what an allergy really is.

As a result, people often think they are allergic to a medication when they may have actually been experiencing a side effect that isn't truly allergic in nature. So, what does it mean to be allergic to a medication?

An allergy is an inflammatory response to a substance (in this case, a medication or food), that is controlled by your body's immune system. These responses can manifest as rash, itching, facial swelling, or even anaphylaxis (a collection of symptoms that can be severe enough to lead to death).[2]

An allergy is not simply a response to a medication that you find unpleasant, such as dizziness, heartburn, or diarrhea; these are what we call side effects or adverse effects. I still want you to tell your physician about any unpleasant side effects you have experienced from a medication so they can avoid prescribing it if possible. Try to avoid saying you're allergic to a medication if you really aren't. It may unnecessarily limit the medications your physician is able to prescribe.

Alcohol and Drug Use

One time as an intern, I had a patient who suddenly developed profuse sweating, diarrhea, and anxiety after being in the hospital for about two days. I racked my brain over and over again to figure

---

[2] "Allergies," Mayo Clinic, accessed February 19, 2022, https://www.mayoclinic.org/diseases-conditions/allergies/symptoms-causes/syc-20351497.

out what had gone wrong—and I immediately began cardiac and infectious workups.

In the midst of my frantic work, my senior resident calmly tapped me on the shoulder and told me to prescribe the patient methadone because he was going through opiate withdrawal. Our patient had neglected to mention he was taking prescription opiates that he bought illegally. We were able to prescribe him the medications that would help with his withdrawal symptoms, and we also got him to consider rehab after he was discharged.

I can't tell you how many times this scenario has played out with patients who struggle with substance use disorder. Though it may be hard to share the details of addiction, please know that when your care team is not aware of your drug and alcohol use, it can hinder and complicate your care. For example, you could experience dangerous withdrawal symptoms that could have been avoided, the amount of time you spend in the hospital might be extended, and your clinical outcomes can be substantially different from what's expected if your care team isn't aware that they should be treating you for alcohol or drug withdrawal in a timely manner.

Be honest about your alcohol and drug intake. Smoking and vaping habits are also important for us to know about. I sincerely hope that you know that your physician and the rest of the care team are not there to judge you—instead, it's their job to treat you with respect and compassion while helping you by getting you the treatment and support you need.

Bonus Item: Family Medical History

When you come into the hospital, you will be asked about your family's medical history because it will help your physician know what diseases you are at risk for having, the most immediate concerns being heart disease and cancers. I'm calling this a bonus item because although it is helpful information, it is not the most vital piece in the puzzle.

Family history is tough because family is tough. Some people are estranged from their families and have little to no access to the information. Others may be adopted and not know anything about their biological parents. Irrespective of your situation, anything you can give us will be helpful.

Specialized Care Providers

Now, if you are someone with a chronic and/or progressive disease, chances are that you're being followed by at least one medical specialist, or you may be getting one or more special medical interventions. If you are getting specialized treatment for something and have a very specific specialist or specialized care team, please be sure you know who they are and how to contact them. You may be on dialysis, have a rare neurologic disorder, have a cancer, or be a transplant patient. Whatever your situation is, if you're seeing a specialist regularly, you should make available information about how to contact that physician.

It will really aid your hospitalist if they know who your specialists are so that they can reach out to them for more information on your current condition and treatment plan. Alternatively, your specialist may prefer to be the one caring for you and help facilitate a transfer to their hospital if you are at a different facility.

Similarly, if you always go to hospital X, but for some reason, you ended up at hospital Y, it will be of benefit to you if you try and go back to hospital X for continuity of care and access to your specialized care team. When you're in an ambulance, it is likely they're going to take you to the nearest hospital, which is why it's crucial that you communicate where your specialists are and what your preferred hospital is when you get to the emergency department. Additionally, if for some reason you can't communicate for yourself, ensure your loved ones also know the name of your usual hospital and your specialists so they can help advocate for you.

To see how such a scenario would play out, imagine you have had a heart transplant and your cardiologist and cardiothoracic surgeon are at the local University Hospital, but you ended up at a different hospital. If that's the case, you can ask to be transferred to your usual hospital. Literally tell the emergency medicine physician, "Please transfer me to University Hospital. That's where my care team is."

The physicians in the emergency department will proceed to stabilize you first, then check with University Hospital to make sure you can be accepted there. Unfortunately, it's not always guaranteed that you will be able to be transferred to your preferred hospital if there are not open beds to accommodate you or if your request isn't deemed medically necessary by the other hospital.

So, why does it matter which hospital you are being admitted to?

If you are someone who has experienced multiple admissions at a specific hospital or you receive the majority of your care within one medical system, then your specialists—along with your medical records—will be more readily available at that hospital or system. This means your usual hospital will have better access to your information, the people who are used to treating you, and the specialized things you may need.

Now, if you're on vacation and end up at somewhere like the Machu Picchu Hospital, that's a more peculiar case. But if you do have the opportunity to be transferred to the place where you get most of your care, you can request to go back there.

Special Medical Therapies

This area is a simple but important one. Tell us all the very specific things you do to manage your chronic conditions so we can accommodate you as best as possible.

For example, if you wear a CPAP to sleep at night, tell your hospitalist so that they can order one for your use while in the hospital. Or if you're on a special diet due to your medical condition (e.g., people with celiac disease must eat a gluten-free diet), tell your physician this when you are being admitted so that they can order the correct foods for you.

The finer details will not only improve your outcomes, but also make a difference in your general experience at the hospital.

Medical History Template

Medical History

Name_____

Current Medications

Name of Medication	Dose	Frequency/ Timing	Still Taking (Y/N)	Indication
Ex: Metoprolol	50 mg	Twice a day	Yes	Blood Pressure

Medical Issues

Active Medical Issue	Treating Doctor	Taking Medication
Ex: High Blood Pressure	Dr. ABCD	Yes

Surgeries

Surgery	Surgeon's Name	Date
Ex: Back Surgery	Dr. EFGH	1/1/2010

Allergies

Medication/Food Name	Reaction	Severity
Ex: Penicillin	Rash	Mild

Social

Alcohol use: Yes/No. How many days a week? How many drinks per day?

_____

_____

_____

Tobacco use: Yes/No. Describe.

_____

_____

*Be prepared to discuss any other drug/substance use openly with your physician.

Family History

Condition	Relative
Ex: Stroke	Mother

What to Bring to the Hospital

So you're on your way to the hospital. Below, you'll find some necessities I recommend you bring along.

1. Identification/Insurance
2. Important documents, such as advance directives, portable medical orders
3. Personal assistance items, such as eyeglasses, hearing aids, dentures
4. Specialized Medications
5. Go-Bag—Is it possible?

Identification/Insurance

This is a fairly self-explanatory one. The registration team will need to know who you are, so bring some form of identification such as your driver's license and your insurance cards. If you have more than one type of health insurance, bring the cards for each insurer. Also, be sure to bring the insurance cards for your prescriptions. Though you may not need all of the different health insurance information to check in, you may need them for discharge planning, so it is good to have it in the system.

Each hospital has their own protocols on how to identify patients who are brought in unconscious and/or without any identification, so don't spend too much time worrying about this scenario.

Important Documents

During a hospitalization, it is not uncommon for patients to need the assistance of another person who has been designated to serve as a decision-maker. Nor is it uncommon for people to have delineated their personal preferences around what type of care they are willing to accept and what limits on treatments they want to set.

An advance directive (also called a living will) is a legal document that clearly states your care preferences and who you want to be making medical decisions for you if you are not able to do so yourself. Having this document available during a hospitalization will ensure that your wishes are carried out at all times.

Portable medical orders are known by different names across the U.S. (e.g., California uses POLST, Massachusetts uses MOLST),[3] but the content of these orders is the same. A portable medical order is a document that serves as a set of medical orders to carry out your wishes around end-of-life treatments and emergency resuscitative procedures. These are medical orders for the physicians and nurses involved in your care and should be honored as such. If you have a POLST/MOLST, it is a good idea not only to keep a copy in a readily accessible location but also to be sure your healthcare proxy and PCP have copies as well.[4]

POLST Programs by State

National POLST Form

---

3   "National POLST Maps," National POLST, accessed February 20, 2022, https://polst.org/programs-in-your-state/.

4   "About POLST," National POLST, accessed February 20, 2022, https://polst.org/about/.

Personal Assistance Items

Being in the hospital without your glasses, dentures, or hearing aids will only lead to more frustration. Imagine not being able to read a consent form from a surgeon or hear what your nurse is telling you during a medical emergency. Many people avoid bringing these items to the hospital out of fear that they will get lost. But being without the devices that help you navigate the world will just limit your ability to be an informed and active participant in your hospitalization. Having a system to keep track of your personal items will decrease the chances they will be lost. For example, keep a small bag with your name on it and place your glasses, hearing aids, etc. in that bag anytime you go for a test. This way you are not asking the technologists or transporter to hold your personal items. Canes, walkers, and wheelchairs will be provided, but you can also bring your own.

Specialized Medications

If you are taking a very rare or very expensive medication, it may be best to bring it along with you to the hospital. In fact, if you're wondering whether or not to bring a medication—just bring it. It's always better to have the medication and not need it than to have to scramble and find someone to bring it to the hospital for you.

You may be surprised by this suggestion and wonder, "Doesn't the hospital have all the medicines I need?" The answer is typically yes. Hospitals usually have the medicines you need, but in the case of infrequently prescribed medications or ones that are very expensive, they may not be on the hospital's formulary (list of medicines a hospital purchases for its pharmacy). Keeping these rarely used medications in stock may not be feasible for a hospital, so bringing your own medication is the best way to be sure you will get it in a timely manner. If you do not have your specialized medication with you when you are being admitted to the hospital, you can ask someone to bring it in for you later on.

A Go-Bag—Is It possible?

For pregnant people, it's common practice to prepare a hospital bag, chock-full of everything they'll need during their stay. Sometimes, they'll organize this bag and set it aside weeks in advance of their due date in case an unexpected hospitalization occurs. Makes sense, right?

If you find yourself in the hospital regularly, I would highly recommend assembling a go-bag for yourself—it'll take a lot of pressure off you and your loved ones if you unexpectedly fall ill. However, I wouldn't waste any mental headspace on a go-bag if you're not visiting the hospital often. *As long as you can provide the four important pieces of medical history we talked about earlier, especially what medications you're taking, and have the prior-mentioned documents, essentially, you should be covered.*

This go-bag recommendation does, however, come with an asterisk. If you do decide to get a go-bag together, please just pack the basics (i.e., flip-flops for the shower, personal hygiene stuffs, a pen, paper, phone charger) and don't plan on furnishing the hospital with your favorite knickknacks. Bringing extra things and overcrowding a room can be a safety hazard.

What Are the Different Types of Hospitals?

In 2021, there were 919,559 hospital beds in the United States.[5] It may seem like a lot, but in actuality not all hospitals are the same, and thus all these hospital beds are not going to be able accommodate every type of patient. It is not possible for every hospital to have every specialist, offer every type of testing modality, or give every type of treatment. Depending on their size and mission, different hospitals will have differing capabilities and cater to different patient populations. Also, hospitals will vary on the level of care that they are able to deliver.

It may not be possible for you to pick the hospital that you are taken to if you're taken in by ambulance or under duress in general, but you should still know some basic information about the different types of hospitals in case you do get a chance to choose. I will share these with you in the next section.

In addition to differing in practice scope and capability, hospitals can also vary in their quality ratings. Information on how hospital quality is judged can be found on the websites of organizations such as the Centers for Medicare and Medicaid Services[6] and the American Hospital Association.[7] Some hos-

---

5   "Fast Facts on U.S., 2021," American Hospital Association, accessed February 20, 2022, https://www.aha.org/statistics/fast-facts-us-hospitals.
6   "Center for Medicare and Medicaid Services," CMS.gov, accessed February 20, 2022, https://www.cms.gov/.
7   "American Hospital Association," American Hospital Association, accessed February 20, 2022, https://www.aha.org/.

pitals will also have special designations or certifications as a hospital that can treat specific illness, such as stroke centers and cancer centers.

> **REAL TALK:**
>
> **HOW WE DETERMINE SAFETY IN THE HOSPITAL**
>
> You may have seen a hospital's safety rating before, but how are safety ratings determined? It really comes down to measuring the number and type of undesired events that occur.[8] Some examples of undesired events are listed below:
>
> - **Iatrogenic infections**: an infection that occurs during a hospitalization
> - **Falls**: slips in the hospital that may or may not result in injury
> - **Medication errors**: the patient is given either the wrong medication or dosage (Medication errors are not the same thing as an adverse effect.)
>
> The types of events that will be measured are set by various agencies and then reported back to be used in calculations that are made public as safety and quality ratings for hospitals.

---

[8] "Errors, Injuries, Accidents, and Infections," Leapfrog Hospital Safety Grade, accessed February 20, 2022, https://www.hospitalsafetygrade.org/what-is-patient-safety/errors-injuries-accidents-infections.

Types of Hospitals- A Hierarchy of Care

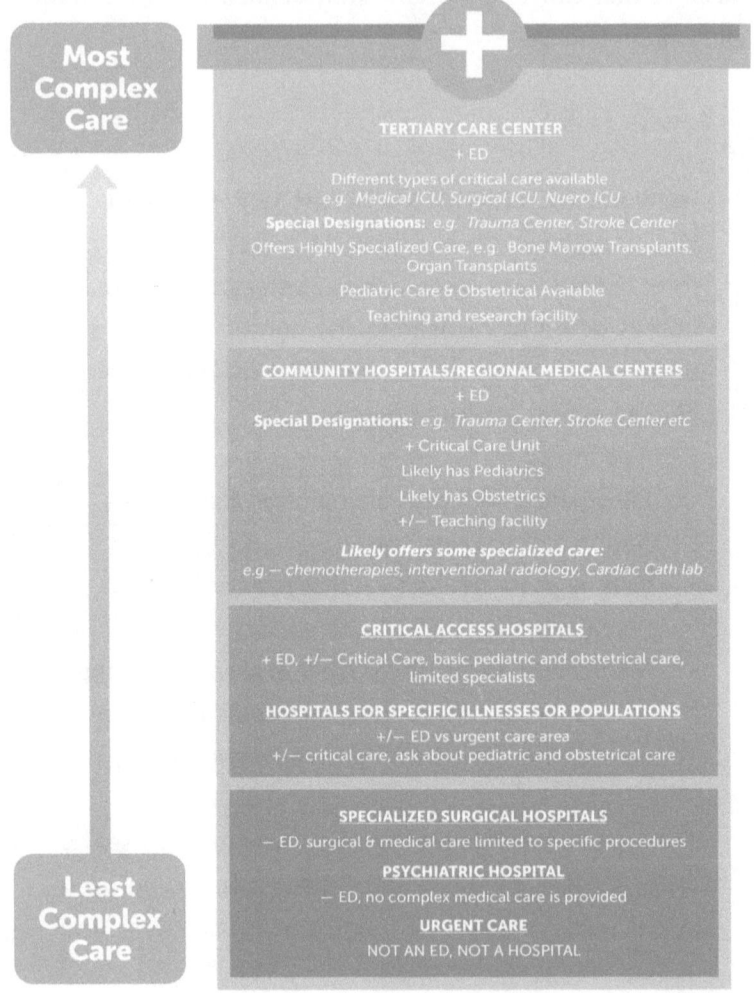

There are many ways to categorize hospitals. The above graphic is how I think of it. I classify hospitals based on the complexity of care and the relative size you can expect the hospital to be. I've placed tertiary care facilities at the top of the diagram as these facilities are able to care for the sickest patients, and this is where you can find some of the most specialized care, including clinical trials. Community hospitals are where the bulk of hospital care is delivered in the U.S. They are able to care for most patients and will be able to transfer any patient who needs more care to a tertiary care hospital. Critical access hospitals are small hospitals in rural communities that do not have access to larger medical centers.

A critical access hospital has 25 beds or fewer and is located more than 35 miles from any other hospital. Although critical access hospitals do not have a wide breadth of medical specialties, they are always able to stabilize and transfer patients to bigger hospitals if needed. They're very much the backbone of rural healthcare.[9]

I describe specialty hospitals as those that care for a select population of patients or a select type of pathology and, therefore, develop the support necessary to care for these highly specialized groups. It is a rather broad category, so here is a short list of hospitals that generally fall under this umbrella: veterans' affairs hospitals, psychiatric hospitals, children's hospitals, and cancer hospitals.[10]

Special Hospital Certifications

Hospitals can apply for certifications proving that they are especially equipped to deliver care for specific types of illness, special patient populations, and have specific services. Being a trauma center is an example of a special certification that you may have heard of. Other types of certifications are stroke centers, cancer

---

[9] "Critical Access Hospitals," Rural Health Information Hub, accessed February 2, 2020, https://www.ruralhealthinfo.org/topics/critical-access-hospitals.

[10] "Specialty Hospitals," American Academy of Orthopedic Surgeons, updated June 2016, https://www.aaos.org/globalassets/about/position-statements/1167-specialty-hospitals.pdf.

centers, or baby-friendly hospitals. Hospitals that have achieved special certifications are going to be able to deliver more robust care for those specific situations than other hospitals. For example, a hospital that is a stroke center will have a neurologist available 24/7, an MRI (magnetic resonance imaging) machine, an intensive care unit (ICU), and the infrastructure—including physical and speech therapists—to care for stroke patients after their initial presentation.[11]

The process that a hospital goes through to achieve a special certification is dictated by whichever organization oversees it and may include more than one such organization. For example, though trauma centers are designated by the state or local municipality, the American College of Surgeons verifies that the surgeons and hospital are able to deliver emergency care and continue all necessary care, such as radiology, ICU care, and so on, for the traumatically injured patients.[12] Also, there are five levels of trauma centers, with a level 1 trauma center being able to deliver the most comprehensive care for more severely injured people, and level 5 trauma centers being able to give basic care to stabilize trauma patients so they can be transferred to another hospital for further care.[13]

Knowing what type of care the hospitals in your area have been certified to deliver will help you know if you are in the right place for the care you need.

---

[11] "Primary Stroke Center Certification," The Joint Commission, accessed March 22, 2022, https://www.jointcommission.org/accreditation-and-certification/certification/certifications-by-setting/hospital-certifications/stroke-certification/advanced-stroke/primary-stroke-center/.

[12] "Trauma Centers," American College of Surgeons, accessed March 22, 2022, https://www.facs.org/search/trauma-centers.

[13] "Trauma Center Levels Explained," American Trauma Society, https://www.am-trauma.org/page/traumalevels.

Part Two: In the Emergency Department

But First, a Few Technicalities

There are some critical decisions you need to make when you are seeking care for an urgent medical need—namely, where you are going and how you should get there.

An Urgent Care Center Is Not the Emergency Department

What exactly differentiates an urgent care center from an emergency department?

The simple-ish answer is that an urgent care center is not able to deliver the same high-acuity care as can the emergency department. An urgent care center is best used for medical issues that need to be treated on the same day but are not life threatening—things like sprains and coughs and rashes. Basic procedures, such as sutures and vaccinations, can also be done at an urgent care center. I want you to think of going to an urgent care center as going to a more intensive doctor's office visit.

On the other hand, an emergency department is staffed and equipped to handle practically every medical issue, from the most basic to very complex and life-threatening situations. ***Emergency departments are supported by a hospital, and patients who require further care will have the support of all the inpatient services available at that hospital, including critical care, surgical, and obstetrical services.***[14] *Furthermore, emergency*

---

14 "Emergency vs. Urgent Care: What's the Difference?," Mayo Clinic, September 3, 2020, https://www.mayoclinichealthsystem.org/hometown-health/speaking-of-health/emergency-vs-urgent-care-whats-the-difference.

departments are staffed by emergency medicine physicians and other healthcare providers who specialize in the treatment of medical emergencies. Depending on who owns and operates the urgent care facility, you may find providers from various medical specialties working there, not just those trained in emergency medicine. Also, an urgent care center will generally close at a certain hour, as opposed to an emergency department that is always open.

> **PRO TIP FOR URGENT CARE:** Try not to go to an urgent care 60 minutes or less before closing.

Arriving in the Emergency Department

There are many ways you can get to the hospital—namely, by calling 911, driving yourself, or being driven by somebody else. More and more, we see people using rideshare apps to get to the emergency department or hospital.[15] If you are choosing to arrive to the emergency department (ED) via ambulance, please be aware that the transportation and care delivered by ambulances are not free. You and your insurer will be billed.[16] Another important thing to know is that arriving by ambulance doesn't guarantee you will be seen before other patients.

Which patients are seen first in the ED depends on how ill-appearing they are and how serious their complaints are. The process of sorting patients based on how quickly they need medical attention is called triage, and providers who work in the ED are

---

15   Leon Moskatel and David Slusky, "Did UberX Reduce Ambulance Volume?," *Health Econ.* 28, no. 7 (July 2019): 817–829, https://doi.org/10.1002/hec.3888.
16   Rod Brouhard, "The Cost of an Ambulance Ride," Verywell Health, May 28, 2021, https://www.verywellhealth.com/why-an-ambulance-costs-so-much-4093846.

experts at triage.[17] The truth is, the person who gets brought in by ambulance and isn't able to wake up and say anything likely needs more immediate attention than the person who arrived by ambulance and is yelling loudly for a physician. Why? Because the unconscious person probably doesn't have a blood pressure high enough for them to be alert and screaming in pain. Thus, the unconscious person is sicker than the patient who is wide awake, alert, and oriented enough to make a commotion.

Whichever way you feel safest getting to the hospital is probably the best way to go. Just understand that your mode of transportation doesn't dictate how quickly you will be seen.

What Is EMTALA??

Time to get your history pants on.

The year was 1986. Picture shoulder pads. Neon. Aerobics. Lots of hair.

After horrible stories came out about people being "dumped" from emergency departments because they were uninsured or on Medicaid, Congress passed the Emergency Medical Treatment and Labor Act (EMTALA) to prevent that situation from ever happening again.[18]

The law says that an emergency department cannot turn away someone without first assessing and, if necessary, stabilizing the person. Basically, they want to avoid people being turned away from the hospital without being assessed for their safety.

---

17   Trisha Torrey, "What Medical Triage Is in a Hospital," Verywell Health, February 20, 2022, https://www.verywellhealth.com/medical-triage-and-how-it-works-2615132.
18   "EMTALA Fact Sheet," American College of Emergency Physicians, accessed February 19, 2020, https://www.acep.org/life-as-a-physician/ethics--legal/emtala/emtala-fact-sheet/#:~:text=The%20Emergency%20Medical%20Treatment%20and,has%20remained%20an%20unfunded%20mandate.

But what does all of this mean for *you*?

EMTALA means that, regardless of your financial situation or insurance status, you will be able to get some care if you are in an ED.

EMTALA essentially means that an emergency department can't turn you away—but it doesn't mean that you won't get a bill, that insurance has to cover your care, or that emergency medicine providers have to do what you say. It just means that the ED has to assess you and make sure that you are medically safe.

Note: Depending on whether or not an urgent care center is owned by a hospital or is a free-standing private practice, it may or may not be required to abide by the guidelines of EMTALA.[19]

Welcome to the Emergency Department

I know how painful and scary entering the emergency department can be, but my hope is that the information you'll receive in this section will help provide some support for you in uncertain times.

First, let's cover the basics:

1. Who will you meet in the ED?
2. What treatments happen in the ED?

Who Will You Meet in the ED?

In the ED, it's likely that in addition to emergency medicine physicians, you will encounter physician assistants (PA) and nurse practitioners (NP). All of these providers are specialized in the assessment,

---

[19] William Sullivan, "When Does EMTALA Apply? The Semantics of Emergency Care," *Emergency Physicians Monthly*, September 15, 2017, https://epmonthly.com/article/emtala-apply-semantics-emergency-care/.

diagnosis, and care of patients who need immediate medical attention. EDs also have nurses, pharmacists, physical therapists, social workers, mental health providers, etc., all working together to help you get as much out of your time in the ED as possible.

One of the main goals of your emergency medicine team will be to determine where you can be safely cared for. If they determine that your condition is not dangerous and it is feasible for you to get continued care either at home or in the doctor's office, you may be able to leave. But if the ED providers determine that you are too sick to leave, they will suggest that you be hospitalized.

For example, when someone comes into the ED with chest pain, the team will make quick work of assessing their presentation and ordering tests to diagnose the cause of the pain, attempting to rule out the most dangerous things, like a myocardial infarction, a.k.a. a heart attack. If a heart attack is diagnosed or there is more testing necessary to determine what is causing the pain, then the ED provider will coordinate further care with the cardiologist and the hospitalist, and the patient will be admitted to the hospital. If the ED team determines that the chest pain is not dangerous and is from something like a pulled muscle or bad heartburn, then the patient will be discharged home with all the instructions and prescriptions needed to alleviate their pain. Emergency medicine professionals have done a lot of work and research to learn how to quickly determine what is truly dangerous and what isn't so that they can know when it's safe for you to go home and when you should stay for more care.

What Treatments Happen in the ED?

The point of the emergency department is to assess and stabilize you for the next place you can continue your care, whether that be in the hospital or at home.

That being said, you may wonder what actually happens in the ED. Here is a very short, and in no way exhaustive, list of medical treatments that are carried out in the emergency department:

- **Critical medications**: medicines necessary to stabilize your vital signs
- **IV fluids**: fluids given intravenously to treat low blood pressure and dehydration
- **Oxygen**: delivering supplemental oxygen when a patient is having difficulty breathing
- **Antibiotics**: given either in pill form or intravenously to immediately treat an infection
- **Blood transfusions**: donor blood is given to stabilize a patient with a dangerously low red blood cell count and/or active bleeding
- **Crisis mental healthcare**: for example, assessing a suicidal patient
- **Sutures**: stitches to repair lacerations
- **Trauma care**: immediate assessment, stabilization, and treatment after an accident

The number one priority for the ED is always your safety. This attention typically includes stabilizing the most immediate medical issues, and after that, the next focus will be your comfort and further planning.

NOTE ON OBSTETRICS AND THE ED
Emergency departments are capable of handling obstetrical emergencies, including active labor. However, many hospitals with an obstetrics department triage and treat these patients in a different area of the hospital, in what may be considered an obstetrical ED. It is expected that patients in labor or with any other obstetrical concern report to the obstetrical ED. Please check with your obstetrician to find out where you should report if you believe you are in labor or have any other obstetrical emergency.

Your First Conversation in the ED

So, by now you've gone through the whole process of finding a way to get to the hospital, actually got there, checked in, went through triage, waited your turn, and are now being seen. What now?

This is the moment where you're going to have your first conversation with your care team in the emergency department, so it's an important one. The stress of being sick and in the ED makes it easy to forget details, give unnecessary information, and do a poor job of painting the big picture—which is why in this chapter I'm going to help you get ready for this first conversation with your emergency medicine team.

It Feels Like the First Time

Some of these are questions, whereas some are advice. You should be able to have clear and concise responses for your providers, but fear not if you don't yet. We can massage your answer into shape together, by focusing on these questions:

- Why did you come to the ED today?
- When was the last time you felt well?
- What have you done to make things better?

Let's get to it!

Why Did You Come to the ED Today?

A big recommendation of mine is to *start with your immediate concern*. Your medical provider will refer to it as your *chief complaint*.[20]

In other words, I'm asking what is the exact reason why you decided to come to the hospital *today, at this moment?* If you have been dealing with an ongoing problem, why is today different from other days? Why is today the day you decided to seek treatment? If this is a brand-new problem, what is so concerning about your problem that you came to seek help at a hospital?

When Was the Last Time You Felt Well?

It's important for your providers to know how long your issue has been going on. If you pinpoint the moment your symptoms began, it can give your provider an understanding of the nature of your illness.

Having experienced symptoms for days versus hours versus minutes can make a big difference in what is considered as a diagnosis. Knowing how long the symptoms have been going on can also make a difference in how you are treated for your symptoms.

For example, if you say, "My face started drooping twenty minutes ago," your ED team may consider stroke as a diagnosis and possibly treatment with tissue plasminogen activator (tPA), which can reverse stroke symptoms. Whereas others who are unable to give a clear timeline, such as someone saying, "My wife said that my face was drooping at breakfast, but I'm not sure when it started," may not qualify for tPA treatment. Furthermore, a longer

---

20 Michael M. Wagner et al., "Chief Complaints and ICD Codes," in *Handbook of Biosurveillance* (Cambridge, MA: Academic Press, 2006), https://doi.org/10.1016/B978-012369378-5/50025-9.

timeline for your symptoms, such as "I've noticed my face getting weaker over the past few months," may make your ED providers concerned about more slow-growing problems, not something acute like a stroke.

What Have You Done to Make Things Better?

Similarly, an effective direction to take is to talk about what you've done to make things better. For example, what medications have you taken to alleviate your discomfort? Does a specific position make your pain worse? Do specific foods cause more nausea or diarrhea?

Answers to these questions can provide a lot of information and may help to get closer to a diagnosis.

REAL TALK:

DON'T TAKE IT PERSONALLY

Have you ever noticed doctors constantly interrupt you? A 2018 study concluded that doctors give patients about 11 seconds before interrupting, but don't take it personally![21] They are trying to draw out as much information as possible. The interruptions are not simply because your doctor is trying to move on to the next patient. What's more likely is that they are asking direct questions to help make a diagnosis and treatment plan or to fill in the gaps for something you've already mentioned.

---

21 Naykky Singh Ospina et al., "Eliciting the Patient's Agenda—Secondary Analysis of Recorded Clinical Encounters," *Journal of Internal Medicine* 34, no. 1 (2019): 36–40, https://doi.org/10.1007/s11606-018-4540-5.

Accept That Your Answers Won't Be Perfect

During my time as a medical student, I once spent 30 minutes interviewing a patient. (You can imagine how proud I was after reporting a near essay to my team.) But when the attending physician and the team followed up with the patient afterward, she suddenly gave them a very different story! She noticed my confusion and explained, "Oh my gosh, I'm so sorry! I didn't lie to you—I just didn't remember everything until after you left!"

Everyone's story changes over time as you start identifying what is important and can fill in the gaps with the finer details. That's okay! Give as much information as you can each time you speak to your care team. The complete story will eventually come together.

Your Social History Is Important Too. Please Be Honest

Please tell us the truth about your social behaviors.

If you were drinking alcohol or using any illicit substances, we need to know. If you didn't use protection during intercourse, we need to know. If you've traveled and may have been exposed to an infectious disease, we need to know. Getting a complete social history can make a difference in getting to a diagnosis and also in making a safe medical plan for your hospitalization. For example, it is not an uncommon occurrence for a patient to suddenly become sick on the third or fourth day of their hospital stay. This unexpected clinical change can be a sign of withdrawing from alcohol, and it complicates and prolongs a hospitalization. If your physician can plan ahead to help you manage withdrawal symptoms, you can avoid unnecessary setbacks and discomfort.

Remember that your health record is privileged information, as are your conversations with your healthcare providers, so you have nothing to lose by being honest.

Medication Reconciliation

Have you ever heard of the phrase *medication reconciliation*? If you have no ties to the medical world, you're probably drawing a blank. That's very normal—most people don't know a thing about this very important process!

But it just so happens that medication reconciliation is one of the most important things that occurs during a hospitalization. It is the practice where your physician reviews a list of every medicine you were taking before you came to the hospital and then decides which of those you should continue taking during your hospitalization. This process is repeated again when you are being discharged, and it may occur repeatedly during your hospitalization if you have a surgery or at any other time when your care team makes a big transition.[22]

Remember that I emphasized how critical it is to know your medications, the dosage, and how often you take them? The purpose was to prepare a complete list for the medication reconciliation process—and your safety. I want your physician and care team to know what you're taking so that they can appropriately continue it through the hospitalization or stop it if necessary. If a complete and accurate medication reconciliation is not done, patients run the risk of missing important chronic medications, receiving duplicate medicines, or taking medications that could negatively affect them. For your convenience, I've inserted a form on page 43 that you can update with your personal information.

---

[22] "Medical Reconciliation to Prevent Adverse Drug Events," Institute for Healthcare Improvement, accessed February 19, 2022, http://www.ihi.org/Topics/ADEsMedicationReconciliation/Pages/default.aspx.

I've seen what happens when a medication reconciliation is incomplete or inaccurate. Say, for example, that for whatever reason, a patient's anti-seizure medication does not get continued during their hospitalization. Then, when day three or four of their hospitalization rolls around, the patient has a sudden and seemingly random seizure. A mad rush ensues, where the care team does everything they can to figure out what's going on. Then, the hospitalist will get a call from the patient's partner who says, "Did you give them their seizure medication?" This may sound farfetched, but it isn't. Your physicians can only make the best care plan if they have complete information, and it starts with your list of medications and the medication reconciliation process.

Let me walk you through a demonstration of your hospitalist's thought process while completing the medical reconciliation process on admission. Let's say a patient comes into the hospital with an abnormally low blood pressure, but they also take a medication called metoprolol, a very commonly prescribed medicine that lowers blood pressure by slowing down the heart.

Knowing about the metoprolol, the hospitalist may decide it's not safe for the patient to take the metoprolol while in the hospital. They could even conclude that the patient should stop taking it afterward too. Either way, the patient will be leaving the hospital with a whole new set of instructions and prescriptions, which may or may not include metoprolol.

Now that you understand the importance of the medication reconciliation process, I want to explain the possible reasons you may not get your usual medication.

- **Safety**: It may not be safe to give you your chronic medications in the hospital because of how ill you are or because a new medical concern has arisen, such as impaired kidney function. Another reason you would not get your regular medicine is the possibility that your chronic medication can interact with another medication you are getting in the hospital.

- **Lack of medical necessity**: If a medication isn't really necessary for you to take regularly or necessary now that you're in the hospital, it may occur that you are not prescribed that medicine. Examples include nutritional supplements, weekly or monthly dosed medications, topical lotions or creams for noncritical skin conditions.
- **Hospital's formulary**: Every hospital's pharmacy has contracts with companies who supply their medications and will not be able to carry every medication ever made. Very specialized or new medications may not be available at the hospital yet. And common alternatives to your regular medication may be given instead. *See "What to Bring to the Hospital" in "Part One: Pre-Day One" on page 20.*

Understandably, a change in the dosage of a medication or withholding of it entirely can make a patient have doubts and apprehensions—but there's usually a logical justification for why the change occurs, so feel free to ask why you aren't getting your regular medicines.

List your prescriptions in the template provided on page 16.

Medication Reconciliation: Admission List

Name	Taking at Home	Continue in Hospital	New During Hospitalization
Ibuprofen	Yes	No	
Metoprolol	Yes	No	
Loratadine	Yes	No	
Ceftriaxone	No	___	Yes
Acetaminophen	No	___	Yes

PRO TIP FOR MEDICATIONS: If your hospital's pharmacy doesn't carry your specific medication, remember that you can bring it in yourself.

Should I Stay, or Should I Go?

Once the emergency medicine physician determines that you should be hospitalized, if you are not going to the critical care unit or having surgery, the next provider you're going to talk to will likely be a hospitalist (so, someone like me!). A hospitalist is a physician (PAs and NPs can also be a part of the hospital medicine team) who has been trained in either internal medicine or family medicine to treat acutely hospitalized adults. When the hospitalist comes along, their job will be to talk to and assess you, review your labs, radiology, etc., and then make a medical plan for you, writing a bunch of other medical orders.

One of the sentiments I often hear in this stage is "I don't want to be in the hospital; I want to go home." So, what do you do if you find yourself asking, "Should I stay, or should I go?" when you're given the option to enter the hospital as an inpatient?

A great place to start when trying to answer this question is to ask yourself and your hospitalist, "What is being accomplished by my staying in the hospital?" There should be a clear explanation as to why you need to be in the hospital and what they are doing for you that cannot be accomplished anywhere else. Getting this information will allow you to answer the critical question, "Should I stay, or should I go?"

If you're thinking that you'd prefer going home but can't decide, consider these questions:

- Is it safe to leave the hospital in the physical state that you are currently in?
- Is your pain/nausea/vomiting or any other concerning symptom controlled, or will you need to come back because of worsening or uncontrolled symptoms?
- Will you be able to get and take necessary medications at home?
- Will you have a medical (e.g., wound care, medicines) and emotional (e.g., friends, family) support system to continue your care after leaving the hospital?
- Will you have access to the physicians you need to see if you leave, like your primary care physician or any specialists?
- Will you be able to safely and consistently access food and water?
- Are you physically safe in your home?
    - Are there stairs you need to go up or down?
    - Will you be able to sleep where you usually sleep?
    - Can you move easily around your home in your current condition?

If you can't answer *yes* to *all* of those questions, then it is probably not safe for you to leave the hospital. That being said, no one can force you to stay in the hospital except if you have been placed on a psychiatric hold or if you are not the person making your medical decisions. If you decide to leave the hospital despite counseling from the ED and/or hospital medicine team, then it is likely that you will be asked to sign documentation that you are leaving despite your team's medical advice that you stay. This action is also known as *leaving against medical advice* (leaving AMA).[23] Some studies show that people who prematurely leave the hospital with an AMA discharge are at increased risk of returning to the hospital, having a poor outcome, or even dying.[24] Please take your time to discuss all options with your care team prior to leaving AMA.

---

23 Trisha Torrey, "Leaving the Hospital Against Medical Advice," Verywell Health, October 27, 2021, https://www.verywellhealth.com/choosing-to-leave-the-hospital-against-medical-advice-2614871.

24 David J. Alfandre, " 'I'm Going Home': Discharges Against Medical Advice," *Mayo Clinic Proceedings* 84, no. 3 (March 2009): 255–260, https://doi.org/10.1016/S0025-6196(11)61143-9.

A Fork in the Road

The emergency department is not a place to stay for a long time. It's a place to be assessed and receive any appropriate treatments, but then you move on to your next stop. If your care team has discharged you from the ED, this means that the emergency medicine providers have assessed you and feel that it's safe for you to go home. This doesn't mean that you are not sick. It just means that you do not need to be hospitalized and that it is safe to get any further care in an outpatient setting. If you are prescribed medications, need a referral to a specialist, or need to be set up with in-home medical services, the case manager or social worker in the ED will help ensure you get these things. After any visit to the ED, be sure to schedule an appointment with your PCP to follow up on the issue.

If you are being discharged from the ED but do not feel safe to leave, then request to speak with the emergency medicine physician charged with your care, and discuss your concerns with them. Have an open and honest conversation with your provider and nurse to explain why you are uncomfortable going home. ED nurses are really great advocates for their patients, so utilize your nurse to help you communicate with the providers and come up with a plan that you feel comfortable with.

If you do need to be admitted to the hospital, then you'll be assessed by the inpatient medical team and eventually moved to another part of the hospital where your acute hospitalization will continue. The point is, long-term care does not happen in the emergency department, and you are ready to move on to the next phase of your care.

REAL TALK:

LEAVING AGAINST MEDICAL ADVICE (AMA)

Leaving AMA means that you have decided to leave the hospital despite the fact that your medical team believes the safest thing for you to do is to stay in the hospital for further treatment. Leaving AMA doesn't just happen in the emergency department—you may leave AMA at any point in a hospitalization.

If you choose to go, leaving AMA doesn't have to be a contentious process; you can and should try to leave in a calm and organized manner to ensure you get the medications and support you'll need after you've left. After discussion with your care team, if you feel that you must leave AMA, you will be required to sign paperwork acknowledging that you are going to leave the hospital despite being advised to stay. After that is done, you can gather your things and leave. The situation specific to your case will determine if and what types of medications your physician is able to prescribe to you when you leave AMA and what type of support services you can access after leaving the hospital AMA.

People leave AMA for a myriad of reasons, but if you are considering leaving solely because of a fraught relationship between you and the doctor or nurse (or anyone at the hospital), I would recommend trying other ways of remedying the situation. Try not to allow personality differences to be the reason you cut short a hospitalization.

Part Three: Day One

Admission and Stabilization

At this point, you've officially moved on from the ED and have transitioned into your new, temporary home, either the general medical floors or the ICU. Because I am a hospitalist, my work is focused on the general medical floors, so we will not be talking about the ICU in this book.

The goal of day one is really admission and stabilization—in other words, it's time for you to be "tucked in." Your hospitalist is going to spend their time and efforts making sure that you're clinically stable and safe, meaning that your vital signs (heart rate, blood pressure, temperature, respiratory rate, oxygenation) are within safe parameters.

They will also want to make sure you are comfortable, which is usually indicated by the amount of pain/discomfort a patient is in. There are several ways to address pain and discomfort (medications, interventional procedures, wound care, pillows, hot/cold packs, and so on), so you may be prescribed one or a combination of these. Overall, on day one, your care team is really looking for big outliers that need to be immediately addressed, especially if they can cause you to get sicker.

To demonstrate this concept, let's say you came into the hospital because you passed out. The first set of labs and images that your physicians are going to do will be geared toward your safety (directly after the event). Their focus likely means they're going to do x-rays to make sure you haven't fractured anything, a CT scan to check for intracranial bleeding if you hit your head, or some blood work to look for any urgent issues that are causing you to pass out.

Let's pretend they discovered you had such a low red blood cell count (a severe anemia) that it caused you to faint. The next step they'll take is to give you a blood transfusion so that they can ensure that you are safe (i.e., won't pass out again). Make sense?

After your physician is comfortable that you are safe, they will start making a longer-term plan for your care.

You now know the purpose of day one.

REAL TALK

KNOW WHO IS WHO

The patient communication board is a bulletin board located in your room that provides information about the care plan at a glance. These boards can be updated by any member of your care team, and you should feel free to add to it as well. Be sure to ask each provider to list their name and role in your care on the communication board. If you are able to get a business card from each provider that is a big win, but shouldn't be expected.

Example of a communication board

Big Goals and Little Goals

It is my practice to always ask patients, "What is your goal for this hospitalization?" because a patient's goal can differ from what I, as their physician, may think it is. I've learned that it is important to always address the issue that's bothering a patient the most, in addition to what I see as the most pressing medical concern. Over the years, I've found this practice helps me make a more personal connection with patients and strengthens the therapeutic relationship. Knowing their goals for a hospitalization also gives me an understanding of what someone's longer-term goals are and how realistically they can be achieved.

That being said, when I ask that question and hear, "I want to get better," a small part of me gets frustrated. *Better* isn't particularly informative. Therefore, if a patient says, "I want to get better," my next question is always, "Well, what does *better* mean to you?" That way I can really drill down and find out what is of value to them, because everybody comes to the hospital with different experiences of illness and expectations of cure.

Day one is where I want you to understand the concept of setting big goals and little goals so that you can create some of your own. When I bring up little goals, I'm discussing more day-to-day things, issues that can be solved in a day, or answers that can be found in a day. Little goals may focus on subjects like pain control, movement, test results or personal feelings. As far as quantity goes, I recommend you think of, write down, and speak to your care team about one to three little goals a day.

Alternatively, big goals are your overarching hopes for the end of your hospitalization and what you want to accomplish by then.

Big goals typically require much more coordination and input from a lot of people. I recommend having two to three for your entire hospitalization and addressing one or two a day.

For example, maybe a patient came to the hospital because he has a severe headache, so the big goals of his hospitalization are to have his headache stop and find out why his headache is so severe—which is a lot more informative than "I want to get better."

Big Goal #1: I would like my headache relieved.
Big Goal #2: Get a diagnosis for why my headache is so bad.

The reason why I differentiate between big goals and little goals and not just suggest you make a general goals list is because, chances are, you are spending multiple days in the hospital. Over that time period, you're bound to have smaller aches, pains, or questions that need to be addressed to help you achieve your overarching big goals—and every goal matters. Every tiny goal, thought, or concern you have is a chance for your care team to show up for you and help you accomplish something. And they want to do just that!

Going back to our friend with the headache, on the second day of his hospitalization, he is nauseous. He would create little goals for the day:

Little Goal #1: Control my nausea.
Little Goal #2: Eat a meal.

So, as we discuss big and little goals, remember to be very specific when you think about yours. Moreover, to keep track of your progress and advocate for yourself, write down your big and little goals every day, and tell them to your physician.

Saying something like "Today, I want to have a bowel movement and walk down the hall," can make a huge difference in how you view your day in the hospital. The difference is because you're more likely to accomplish that specific goal and, thus, feel better and see that your care is moving forward.

If, for some reason, your care team isn't able to help you reach your goals one day, ask them why, because you'll still be gathering useful information. "Dr. Nugent, why didn't all those laxatives work for me yesterday?" can lead to an open conversation that leads to different medicines, tests, or physical exam maneuvers.

The following questions are a great place to help you start your list of little goals:

- Are you comfortable today?
- Have you gotten out of bed/taken a shower/had a bowel movement?
- Are you waiting to have a specific test or to get test results?
- Did you see the specialist you expected?
- Do you understand your care plan?

Last, here's an illustration of helpful big goals. Let's say you came to the hospital because of a large lump on your neck, and you don't know what it is. Some appropriate big goals include the following:

Big Goal #1: Figure out what the mass is.
Big Goal #2: Create a plan that outlines what the next steps are after I leave the hospital.

A less useful big goal here would be "Get my cancer cured," if that's what the lump is. The truth of the matter is, there are many things that don't have a "cure." It's an unfortunate truth, and one that's not often portrayed in popular media. We can't cure heart attacks, strokes, or most high blood pressure. We can't cure diabetes. There are some cancers that are curable but also a whole bunch that aren't. But just because there isn't a cure, that doesn't mean there aren't a myriad of treatments that can help you get you back to a place where you're functioning at your best and making plans for continued care.

Now that you know where your big and little goals should fall, my advice to you is to write them down every day and alert your team to them.

I can't speak for all hospitalists, but I usually come up with my own big and little goals for my patients, saying something like, "My goals for you today are for you to sit up in a chair, eat all of your meals, take all of your medications, and meet with the cardiologist to make a plan for your heart disease."

Since I started doing this exercise, my patients report to me that they feel I'm communicating with them more clearly. Furthermore, if their big and little goals don't align with mine, we can talk about why and come to a solution.

REAL TALK:

WHY NUMBER TWO IS NUMBER ONE IN MY BOOK

Let's talk bowel movements. Nothing in life makes people more upset than not being able to have a bowel movement. Having regular bowel movements will help you avoid issues like urinary retention, nausea, and abdominal pain or distension. When you are hospitalized lots of things can cause constipation (e.g., medications, immobility, and acute illness) so be sure to tell your hospitalist about your bowel movements daily.

Having regular, consistent bowel movements will help you avoid complications that can prolong a hospitalization, which is why I recommend you have it as one of your little goals every day.

Code Status and Advance Directive

Picture this: You're watching an episode of your favorite soapy hospital drama. Dr. Gorgeous Man is on rounds when all of a sudden, one of his patients goes limp, and the nurse cries out, "He's in cardiac arrest!"

The hunky hospitalist, with his stoically handsome face, yells, "Code blue! Code blue!" and controlled chaos ensues. A swarm of doctors and nurses rush into the room, then a dramatic version of CPR occurs while someone is crying in the corner.

I'm sure you've wondered in those moments, "What does *code blue* even mean?"

In this case a code blue is the Hollywood depiction of a cardiac or respiratory arrest, meaning that the heart has stopped beating or that breathing has stopped. It is one of many hospital "codes"—monikers that allow the staff to communicate about various emergencies in the hospital with privacy and consistency over the intercom or paging system.

Ironically, *code blue* is rarely used in a hospital because everyone who doesn't live under a rock knows it means trouble. Could you imagine if we yelled, "Code blue for Mr. Smith in room 5101!" on the loudspeakers? It would be terrible!

For this reason, and for patient privacy, each hospital actually has its own set of codes. I've worked in hospitals that use a rainbow of colors for their hospital emergency codes, while others used numbers or a mix of various other monikers.[25]

The Hollywood depiction of a cardiac or respiratory arrest is very gripping, but it is also a bit misleading. One of the major things that Hollywood glosses over is that you have full control over your code status. Code status equates to medical orders that dictate the care delivered in the case of a cardiac and/or respiratory arrest—and the order is made *by you*.

It doesn't seem this way on TV, but resuscitative measures are only attempted in the hospital if a patient or their decision-maker has stated that they would want those things to happen. People don't just go around screaming, "CODE BLUE," in the hall for every patient; in fact, code status is discussed early and often during a hospitalization, and resuscitation efforts only happen to those who have consented to such treatments.

Every hospital I've worked in has required that I have a discussion about code status with every patient on every admission, so expect to be asked about it. Whatever your response is to the code-status question, I understand that it is a very personal decision driven by a multitude of things—such as religious beliefs, known medical illness, prior experiences, fear of pain, belief in medical technologies, and so on. Also, unlike an advance directive (which we'll get into soon), a person's code status can change from hospitalization to hospitalization and at any time during their stay, so don't worry about picking a "permanent" code status.

To summarize, when you get asked for your code status, your hospitalist is basically asking what you want to be done if anything like a code blue happens to you.

---

25 Melissa C. Stöppler, " 'Code Blue,' 'Code Black:' What Does 'Code' Mean?" WebMD, January 15, 2020, https://www.webmd.com/a-to-z-guides/code-blue-code-black-what-does-code-mean.

Below, I will give you some information and a list of questions for you to answer that will help you think about your code status. It's usually not an easy thing to have a conversation about, so please take your time to get comfortable and pull your loved ones near before continuing.

How to Think About Code Status

My speech when I ask a patient about their code status tends to go something like this: "The next question I'm going to ask you is not because I think anything bad is going to happen but because I have to have your answer on the books so I know what you want done in case an emergency happens here in the hospital. Have you ever considered what you would want done in the event that either your heart stopped beating or you have stopped breathing?"

Please know this: When you are asked this question, it is not tantamount to asking whether or not you want to die during your hospitalization. I've had it happen to me numerous times, when I ask an elderly patient about code status, their adult children turn and say, "She's asking whether or not you want to die, Mom/Dad." That's definitely not what I was getting at!

Here's another common misconception I want to dispel: Resuscitation from cardiac or respiratory arrest will automatically end with a patient in a vegetative state, as I often get the response, "I don't want to be a vegetable, Doc." It's not true, nor is that what your code status is meant to address. Attempting resuscitation in the case of respiratory or cardiac arrest solely means we will try to get your heart beating again, or you breathing again, so that additional medical treatments can be delivered for whatever caused the cardiac or respiratory arrest. What happens after that is up to you as dictated by either an advance directive or the person designated to be your decision-maker if you are not able to participate in decision-making afterward.

Let's Talk About Your Code Status

I know that there is nothing easy about discussing this subject matter, which is why I've created some space for you below to work through these tough questions. That way, you can be prepared before your hospitalization, feel confident in your decision, and know how to approach the conversation again if needed.

Imagine a situation when your nurse walks into the room and notices that you're unresponsive. She assesses you and finds that either your heart is beating in an unstable way, or that your breathing is very labored and that your oxygenation is worsening. At that moment, what would you want your nurse to do?

- a. *Run into the hallway and yell, "Code Blue," so that the entire medical team will come and do CPR, etc.*
- b. *Call the doctor so they can assess you and see what can be done to help, which could include helping you be comfortable if it is determined that you may soon die?*

Start by writing down your immediate thoughts on how you would respond to that situation.

_____
_____
_____

Why did you choose your answer?

_____
_____
_____

What are you hoping will happen?

_____
_____
_____

Why are you hoping those things will happen?

_____
_____
_____

What if the code blue doesn't result in a stable heartbeat or if you're not able to safely breath on your own?

_____
_____
_____

That was deep and heavy. Good work.

Now that you have an idea of what you want, let's crystallize it with some medical jargon. As we move through the more technical terms, you have the option of jotting down your thoughts, responses, affirmations, or rejections.

Please note that you don't have to know the official terminology for these procedures. My only goal here is for you to have a sense of each treatment, not for you to memorize medical terms and recite them to your doctor. All you need to be able to do is describe them—your doctor will take care of the rest.

Chest compressions: This describes the manual process of pressing down in a rapid and rhythmic way on a patient's chest in an attempt to re-create a heartbeat and create blood flow.[26]

_____

_____

_____

Antiarrhythmic medications: Such medications work to correct abnormal heart rates or rhythms that, if continued, may lead to death.[27]

_____

_____

_____

Vasopressor medications: These medications artificially raise blood pressure that is dangerously low.[28]

_____

_____

_____

---

26 Catharine A. Bon, "What Is the Chest Compression Technique for Cardiopulmonary Resuscitation?," Medscape, updated September 15, 2020, https://www.medscape.com/answers/1344081-122913/what-is-the-chest-compression-technique-for-cardiopulmonary-resuscitation-cpr.

27 "Medications for Arrhythmia," American Heart Association, updated September 30, 2016, https://www.heart.org/en/health-topics/arrhythmia/prevention--treatment-of-arrhythmia/medications-for-arrhythmia.

28 Lynn Marks, "What Are Vasopressors?," Everyday Health, December 1, 2015, https://www.everydayhealth.com/vasopressors/guide/.

Intubation: The process of inserting a tube down the throat, through the vocal cords, and into the trachea, allowing air to get to the lungs. The tube is then connected to a ventilator to mechanically re-create breathing and deliver oxygen to the lungs.[29]

Defibrillation: A machine will deliver electric shocks intended to reverse unstable heart rhythms that may lead to death. Despite the common portrayal in movies and television, defibrillation does not treat a flatline. A flatline represents a heart that is not beating because there is no electrical activity (asystole). Defibrillation also cannot treat electrical activity that is not producing a pulse (pulseless electrical activity, or PEA).[30]

Full code: This designation is consent to CPR, vasopressor and anti-arrhythmic medications, electrical shocks, or intubation. Your healthcare proxy will make decisions for you afterwards, if you are unable to do so.[31]

---

29 "Intubation," Cleveland Clinic, September 24, 2021, https://my.clevelandclinic.org/health/articles/22160-intubation.
30 Amandeep Goyal et al., "Defibrillation," StatPearls, updated February 7, 2022, https://www.ncbi.nlm.nih.gov/books/NBK499899/?msclkid=b3889631a61211ec9ffdbe1021ab4e33.
31 Viral G. Jain et al., "Code Status Reconciliation to Improve Identification and Documentation of Code Status in Electronic Health Records," *Applied Clinical Informatics* 8, no. 1 (2017), https://www.doi.org/10.4338/ACI-2016-08-RA-0133.

Do not resuscitate (DNR): Resuscitative maneuvers and medications will not be attempted. Care will focus on providing medical treatments to ensure comfort and support the patient and family during the process of dying.[32]

It's important to remember that all the maneuvers, medications, and treatments done for cardiac/respiratory resuscitation, are designed to work together. Furthermore, your underlying medical condition will determine how well you are able to tolerate the treatments necessary for such resuscitation. For instance, a person who previously had very healthy lungs but now requires intubation for severe respiratory distress, will likely recover better than a person who has a chronic lung disease and at baseline requires the use of oxygen.

Furthermore, none of the treatments done for cardiac/respiratory resuscitation will reverse a progressive disease process, nor are they curative for whatever is the underlying condition that caused the cardiac or respiratory arrest.

Please understand that all of these maneuvers, procedures, and medications come with their own set of risks in addition to their possible benefits. Everybody should consider for themselves what they are trying to accomplish by choosing their specific code status and discuss the risks versus benefits of a code with their hospitalist, PCP, and loved ones.

---

32 "Do Not Resuscitate Order," Medline Plus, January 12, 2020, https://medlineplus.gov/ency/patientinstructions/000473.htm.

Will I Survive a Code Blue?

It's a scary question, I know, but it's one we must cover. This is another area where I feel that the media's depiction of cardiac and respiratory arrest falls far from reality.

Studies have found that when asked how likely they are to survive a cardiac or respiratory arrest, hospitalized patients believe their chance of surviving a code blue is about 60%.[33] This is a bit higher than what we actually see in the hospital. A large multicenter study of over seventeen thousand patients in the United States, found that about 17% of patients who experience a cardiac arrest in the hospital survive their hospitalization to be discharged.[34] Survival and quality of life after a cardiac arrest tends to depend on how healthy and functional someone was prior to the cardiac arrest.

I'm telling you this information not to scare you but to better inform you. It is my hope that you have some realistic information to refer to as you think and talk about what code status you feel is best for you.

For your reference, here are some common code statuses:

1. **Full code**: Okay to perform CPR, give antiarrhythmic and vasopressor medications, give shocks, or attempt intubation.
2. **Do not resuscitate**: Do not do any resuscitative attempts.
3. **Do not intubate**: Do not put a breathing tube down the throat and do not place on a ventilator, okay to perform

---

[33] L C Kaldjian et al., "Code Status Discussions and Goals of Care among Hospitalised Adults," *Journal of Medical Ethics* 35, no. 6 (June 2009): 338–42, https://doi.org/10.1136/jme.2008.027854.

[34] Mary Ann Peberdy et al., "Cardiopulmonary Resuscitation of Adults in the Hospital: A Report of 14,720 Cardiac Arrests from the National Registry of Cardiopulmonary Resuscitation," *Resuscitation* 58, no. 3 (September 2003): 297–308, https://doi.org/10.1016/s0300-9572(03)00215-6.

CPR, give anti-arrhythmic and vasopressor medications, and give shocks.[35]

Is Do Not Resuscitate (DNR) the Right Answer for Me?

Now that you understand more about what a goes on during cardiac/respiratory resuscitation, and what your options for a code status are, you may have found that you feel differently than you originally thought you would. I know there can be a lot of stigma, fear, and confusion around listing DNR as a code status, so we will take a deeper dive so you can better understand it.

Let's take a look at what *do not resuscitate* means. This may sound obvious, but DNR doesn't mean *do not treat*.[36] Again, I have to bring this misconception up because I've seen the loved ones of many patients tell them, "Don't do DNR. They're just going to give up on you so they don't have to do anything." This false advice has happened at every hospital I've worked in and to every hospitalist I know.

DNR doesn't mean your medical team will just give up. Remember that resuscitative attempts are not cures and do not reverse disease processes, and thus they are not the only treatment given in a hospital. Patients who have chosen DNR as their code status can still receive antibiotics, noninvasive ventilatory support, surgeries, medications, blood transfusions, pain medications, and any other treatment that is medically appropriate. The only treatment that a patient with a DNR code status will not receive is an attempt at cardiac and/or respiratory resuscitation.

---

35   "Understanding Code Status," Munson Healthcare, accessed February 19, 2022, https://www.munsonhealthcare.org/media/file/6581.pdf.
36   Charles Sabatino, "Do-Not-Resuscitate (DNR) Orders," Merck Manuals, updated May 2021, https://www.merckmanuals.com/home/fundamentals/legal-and-ethical-issues/do-not-resuscitate-dnr-orders.

These patients are still going to get the best care possible. And sometimes giving someone the best care possible means not doing these aggressive interventions but instead focusing on ensuring comfort.

To help demonstrate this, let me share a story with you. I was once caring for of a patient who struggled with a long-standing and irreversible illness whose respiratory status continued to worsen during his hospitalization despite assessment by multiple specialists and treatment with various medications and medical interventions. Early one morning his nurse called me to the bedside because she was concerned about how hard he was working to breathe. When I got to the bedside, I immediately noted that his breathing pattern and effort were unstable. He would not be able to safely breathe like that for much longer.

Because he had chosen DNR/DNI as his code status and listed his wife as his medical decision maker, I called his wife to discuss the current clinical situation and make a plan that would respect his desire to avoid resuscitation and intubation. She directed me not to do any more aggressive treatments, and not to transfer him to the ICU. After more discussion we agreed that the most appropriate way to care for him at that time was to focus on helping him be more comfortable rather than continuing with treatments that were not yielding improvement and were prolonging his suffering. After our call, I updated the nurse about the new plan saying, "Let's support him to ensure he passes away peacefully." We gave him various medications for pain and anxiety, including a morphine drip, and his family came to sit with him during his final hours. When this patient died, he was peaceful, comfortable and surrounded by the ones he loved the most. He had received comprehensive care throughout his acute hospitalization, including all the appropriate supports for him and his family during the time that was actively dying.

What About Do Not Intubate?

Sometimes patients tell me, "Do everything, Doctor, just don't put a tube down my throat." I think these patients are (understandably) separating the idea of intubation from that of resuscitation, in the sense that they think intubation is an isolated treatment that can be separated from other things we do for cardiac or respiratory arrest—but it's not.

I've come to understand their confusion because the act of intubation is usually tied with placing the patient on a ventilator, and many people view intubation and the ventilatory machine as life support. That association is why people tend to mentally distinguish intubation from other resuscitative efforts.

In actuality, intubation and cardiac resuscitation go hand in hand. You cannot breathe if you do not have a heartbeat. And you won't have a heartbeat if you can't breathe. I want you to think of the two as a package deal.

I completely understand wanting to avoid suffering from protracted intubation and life-sustaining treatments, so this is where a clear advance directive (we're getting to it—I promise) will be of benefit. Please understand that if you want adequate attempts at resuscitation in the case of a cardiac or respiratory arrest, you may need to be intubated. If you decide to have chest compressions, electric shocks, and anti-arrhythmic or vasopressor medications but do not want to be intubated, you are choosing an incomplete medical treatment and limiting what results the other treatments can yield.

If you are truly against intubation, please go back to the questions earlier in the book and answer them again. This time I want you to focus on what you were trying to achieve by choosing *do not intubate* the first time you answered those questions, and consider how intubation would help or hinder you from achieving those goals.

Planning Ahead: Advance Directives and Healthcare Proxy

An advance directive, also known as a living will, is similar to a code status in the sense that they're both instructions about medical treatments that you are or are not willing to accept.[37] However, they differ in that an advance directive will be much more detailed than your code status, should give more information about specific medical treatments, and should clearly state whom you have chosen to make medical decisions for you if you are not able to do so yourself. Also, unlike your code status, an advance directive is usually outlined prior to hospitalization, may be done in the presence of a lawyer, and will be a physical piece of paper that you can give to the hospital to scan and keep in your record.

Your code status solely focuses on what happens in the case of cardiac or respiratory arrest and can change with every hospitalization based on your preferences for that visit. Advance directives tend not to change often because, in theory, you would have sat down with your loved ones over a large stack of legal papers and had a long conversation about it. Everyone would have to eventually sign, agreeing that the pieces of paper in front of you will be the determinant that directs your care if you cannot speak for yourself.

---

37 "Living Wills and Advanced Directives for Medical Decisions," Mayo Clinic, August 22, 2020, https://www.mayoclinic.org/healthy-lifestyle/consumer-health/in-depth/living-wills/art-20046303.

In short, think of it this way: code status can be in your advance directive, but not the other way around.

The options are virtually endless with advance directives. They can be as short or long as you like. You can accept or decline specific treatments, only allow intubation for a specific amount of time, assign someone to be your proxy, and so on. Regardless of your requests and reasons for them, know that you should never feel pressured to include something in your advance directive that you don't fully agree with.

Discussing how and when you will set up your advance directive is a conversation you should have, if you haven't already, with your loved ones and care team ASAP. If you're someone with a chronic medical condition that's causing you to come back to the hospital over and over again, there is a likelihood that these decisions need to be made—and I always tell patients that the best time to make big decisions is when you are relaxed and don't have to make them under pressure.

If you can avoid having this conversation at the last second, when a doctor is asking for the answer quickly, it will be much easier for you and your loved ones. I've found that most families who wait until they're in an emergency to make decisions about limiting or accepting care rarely feel at ease, particularly if things don't go the way they envisioned.

Healthcare Proxies

A healthcare proxy is a person whom you designate in your advance directive to make decisions for you when you can't make them yourself. The process to designate this person varies state by state and is based on some other factors like local rules, so I can't get into specifics. I can say, however, that you should seek out the specifics on how to complete the process of designating a healthcare proxy. When I talk to people about it, I really try to focus on the meaning of the word *proxy* because I often see people acting not as proxies for their loved ones but rather as medical decision-makers focused on "what is best" for the patients instead of what the patients would have chosen for themselves. Being a substitute for a person means that you are to act exactly as that person would, not do what you want, but rather exactly what they would have wanted.[38]

For instance, if there is a substitute quarterback who calls the plays that he thinks are better for the football team—instead of calling the plays the original quarterback had already designed and practiced with the team—the team might mess up and lose the game. This is exactly the thinking I want you to bring into being someone's medical proxy. You are them. You are to do what they would do, acting exactly as they would—not acting in the way you'd prefer they would. You must choose the action you think best honors the patient's preferences.

Thus, when choosing a healthcare proxy, it's very important that you pick someone whom you trust to understand, respect, and carry out your wishes. Before making your choice, you will also want to make sure you've had clear conversations with the person you are considering for your healthcare proxy about your wishes and that you've gotten confirmation that they will follow through on those desires even if it is personally hard for them. A good healthcare proxy will be able to recognize and be okay with the fact that you may want a different treatment plan for yourself

---

[38] "Health Care Proxies," Medicare Interactive, accessed February 20, 2022, https://www.medicareinteractive.org/get-answers/planning-for-medicare-and-securing-quality-care/preparing-for-future-health-care-needs/health-care-proxies.

than they would choose for you.

Therefore, when you pick your proxy, you should follow these steps:

1. Create your advance directive to give to them to act on your behalf.
2. Sit down with them and clearly outline what your wants are in writing.
3. Give them a copy of your advance directive so they can easily refer back to it. Having this document will relieve them of the emotional burden of making independent decisions as much as possible because you have already written out your wishes.

Being a good proxy could mean that you will have to say, "I want my loved one to be here. If I were the one choosing, I would allow any treatment that would help them, but I know my loved one's wishes are different."

I have the utmost respect for people in that position because it's a really tough job. But usually when I ask a healthcare proxy to make a difficult decision, it's because there's no 100% "right" thing to do, so focusing on the patient's stated goals serves as the beacon for creating a thoughtful care plan.

Accordingly, it's critical that you, the proxy, have the honest dialogue we talked about with the patient prior to becoming a proxy. You need to have clear instructions so that you have to choose as little as possible and, therefore, don't have to bear so much emotional weight. When a proxy has been left with blank instructions to follow, they will sometimes ask me, "Did I do the right thing, Doctor? What would you have done?"

If you need a healthcare proxy, please don't put them in that position. If you are a healthcare proxy, try to avoid being in an ambiguous position by asking as many specific questions as possible before you are needed to act.

The choices you make regarding your code status, advance directives, and healthcare proxy are very personal. Over the years, I've worked with patients who have made decisions about their code status and advance directive I may not have initially agreed with, but ultimately understood, respected, and followed.

My hope is that with all of the new information I've given you, you are able to make a more informed decision regarding code status and advance directives.

Diet

You may have already been able to guess (or have experienced) that hospital food isn't always the best, but why have a whole chapter on it?

Though hospitals have made great efforts to offer more palatable foods, most of the gastronomic experiences in U.S. hospitals would probably rank fairly poorly on Yelp. But it is important to acknowledge that cooking for patients is not an easy task. The hospital's food services have to serve meals that meet a wide array of dietary and medical needs—everything from caloric requirements to textural limitations. The herculean task of feeding hundreds of patients three meals and furnishing them snacks is further complicated by the need to rapidly accommodate change as some patients' diets may need to change daily or even several times in a day.

Having a basic understanding of why you are being served certain food during a hospitalization can help you avoid some common points of frustration and understand why tailoring a patient's food to their specific medical needs is important.

In this chapter, we will cover all the information you need to know about food in the hospital so that you can be prepared for whatever ends up on your plate.

Disease-Specific Dietary Restrictions

When I was a resident, I would worry about my patients' abilities to adhere to specific diets when they were at home. Once, I even asked a patient to let me know when he was going to the supermarket so that I could call him and discuss his shopping in real time (yes, I was overdoing it). He said it was helpful but that I only picked boring foods.

One reason I love being a hospitalist is that for the days of a hospitalization, I get to know everything that happens to a patient, including the food they eat. In general, we all should try to eat a low-fat, low-sodium, and low-sugar diet, but adherence to this type of diet tends to be more mandated than it is voluntary. While you may try your best at home to abide by the dietary restrictions your physician prescribed, in the hospital you are ensured to receive the special diet you need. Therefore, if your physician is trying to control your sodium or sugar intake, you should expect that you'll receive the prescribed type of nourishment during your hospitalization.

We all know how important proper nutrition is in general, but following the diet plan that's been laid out for you in the hospital can really affect how well you feel and how fast you recover.

Here is a list of some of the most commonly prescribed diets you will come across in a hospital. Be prepared to make some changes to how you eat, as there is a possibility that you will need to be on one of these diets.

1. **Diabetic diet**: low sugar, with a consistent amount of carbohydrates in each meal. By controlling the amount of refined sugars and keeping to a fairly steady amount of other types of carbohydrates in each meal, large fluctuations in blood sugars are avoided.[39]
2. **Cardiac diet**: low salt, low fat. Diets high in fat and salt can contribute to cardiovascular disease (think high blood

---

39   "Diabetic Diet," Medline Plus, accessed February 20, 2022, https://medlineplus.gov/diabeticdiet.html.

pressure, stroke, heart attacks). Salt can also contribute to the buildup of fluid in people who have significant heart disease, so it can be necessary to strictly limit the amount of sodium you eat.[40]

3. **Renal diet**: low potassium, low salt, low protein. The kidneys are responsible for managing the electrolyte and fluid balance in the body, so when someone's kidneys aren't working well, it is necessary to manage fluids and electrolytes by limiting the amount of potassium, salt, and protein ingested. It is of particular importance to limit potassium intake, as high levels of potassium can lead to arrhythmias and even cardiac arrest.[41]

4. **Fluid restrictions**: limited amounts of water (including ice) and any other liquids. When your body isn't able to manage its own water balance, one way your physician will do so is via your diet. Fluid-restricted diets are often prescribed to patients who have heart disease, liver disease, or significant kidney disease, such as those who require renal replacement therapy (a.k.a. dialysis).[42]

Although one could file away diet restrictions as minutiae that are hard to stick to, they really are critical to your health. Think of special diets as part of your medication list—they are also prescribed and necessary for you to get and stay healthy.

Therefore, just as you should provide your list of medications

---

[40] "Cardiac Diet," Memorial Sloan Kettering Cancer Center, accessed February 20, 2022, https://www.mskcc.org/experience/patient-support/nutrition-cancer/diet-plans-cancer/cardiac-diet.

[41] "Kidney Diet and Food for Chronic Kidney Disease (CKD)," American Kidney Fund, September 2, 2021, https://www.kidneyfund.org/kidney-disease/chronic-kidney-disease-ckd/kidney-friendly-diet-for-ckd.html.

[42] "Fluid Restricted Diet," Intermountain Healthcare, accessed February 20, 2022, https://intermountainhealthcare.org/ckr-ext/Dcmnt?ncid=520429033.

to your care team on admission, do the same for your diet. Also similar to medications you're taking, be honest about what you're actually eating! Just as you'd tell your doctor if you're taking half the prescribed dose of your pain medication, tell them if you're only following your diet half the time.

You may be surprised to learn that there is actually very little finger wagging when it comes to a patient's poor dietary compliance, as we all realize that sticking to a certain diet is much easier said than done! However, if you are having a difficult time with your diet and want some advice, the hospital is a great place to get it by speaking to the nutritionist or dietitian. Every hospital-based nutritionist I have ever met has been ecstatic to teach patients how to make sound choices for their special dietary guidelines.

NPO

You may see this acronym on the door or hear members on your care team say something like, "This patient is NPO today."

Although it sounds as if they are speaking in code, this acronym's meaning is no secret. It stands for *nothing by mouth*, derived from the Latin phrase *nil per os*. Similar to how it sounds, the NPO order means that a patient shall not be given food or drink by mouth for as long as that order is active. There are varying levels of NPO:

- **Full NPO**: Absolutely no food, liquid, or medications by mouth.
- **NPO except sips and medications**: The patient may only drink a small amount of liquid to take medications. No significant food or liquid should be given when a

patient has this order.
- **NPO except ice chips or sips**: No significant food or drink shall be given, but the patient can munch on a few ice chips here and there. The point of this order is to allow some room to treat the discomfort of dry mouth and hunger with water but to still keep the patient's gastrointestinal (GI) tract clear in case an intervention is warranted.

Anytime an NPO order is given, it's for safety reasons or concerns that eating could worsen your condition, so the NPO order will stay in place until it is safe to eat and drink. For instance, when there is a increased risk of vomiting or aspiration, you may be placed on an NPO order. Aspiration is when food or liquid enters your airway or lungs by accident. Aspiration can lead to complications like pneumonia or low oxygen levels and can even cause you to stop breathing.

Another common reason for a patient to be NPO is the use of anesthesia. Once you're under anesthesia, your gag reflex is significantly diminished, thus increasing the risk of aspirating the food or drink in your stomach. It is much safer to undergo anesthesia if there is no food in your stomach.[43] Thus, the NPO order is critical to avoid aspiration events that can lead to poor, or even deadly, outcomes. Like most instructions in the hospital, if you're directed to follow this order, please do—and don't sneak food. A friend once called me in tears because her surgery was canceled after she admitted to the anesthesiologist that she ate some applesauce and

---

43 "Do You Know…Fasting Guidelines," St. Jude Children's Research Hospital, accessed February 20, 2022, https://www.stjude.org/treatment/patient-resources/caregiver-resources/patient-family-education-sheets/procedures-tests-sedation/fasting-guidelines.html.

sucked on a lollipop while she was waiting. It may sound extreme to cancel a surgery because of applesauce and a lollipop, but it was done to keep her safe.

Here is a quick list of some conditions and procedures that frequently elicit an NPO order:

- Any procedure, surgery, or test that requires any form of sedation or risk of sedation in case of an emergency
- Certain tests and imaging studies will require you to have an empty stomach for optimal results
- Being overly drowsy or confused (aka "altered mental status") to the point that your physician feels that you may not safely coordinate swallowing
- A neurologic or anatomic abnormality that is compromising how well you can swallow
- GI issues such as pancreatitis in which food or liquids could worsen your symptoms or cause pain

Almost every patient I've ever had on the NPO order wants it taken off as soon as possible, which is understandable. Nobody likes feeling hungry. Just remember, although you may be hungry, hunger is temporary, but the consequences of something like aspiration can be much more permanent and debilitating.

Special Food Textures

In addition to controlling the sodium, sugar, potassium, vitamin K, fat, and so on in your diet, your care team may prescribe a specific type of textured food during your hospitalization and perhaps afterward. We often see such prescriptions in cases where an adult may no longer be able to safely manage solid foods or liquids, so they need different textures to safely swallow.[44]

Some conditions that may change your ability to consume regular-textured foods and liquids include the following:

- Strokes that cause problems with swallowing
- Masses that obstruct the throat, or strictures in the esophagus
- Dementia and other changes in one's cognitive abilities that lead to the inability to coordinate the act of swallowing
- Surgeries that change your anatomy or need time to heal prior to returning to regular-textured foods

In such instances, patients may require a diet consisting of only liquids, soft or puréed foods, food that has been chopped up finely, or liquids with thickeners in them.

If your physician has concerns that the texture of your food may need to be altered, they will likely ask a speech pathologist to evaluate your swallowing capabilities. Speech pathologists who are assessing your ability to swallow are focused on safety first. (Again, they're trying to avoid aspiration.)

The speech pathologist will do bedside testing and possibly order additional imaging to determine how well someone is able to swallow different textures. If you end up requiring a change in the texture of your food, your speech pathologist may come back to evaluate you several times during your hospitalization to

---

44 Sik Yin Ong, "All You Need to Know About Texture-Modified Diets," The Care Issue, accessed February 20, 2022, https://www.jaga-me.com/thecareissue/all-you-need-to-know-dysphagia-texture-modified-diets/.

observe whether or not the change will be a lasting one based on how you're progressing.[45]

Artificial Nutrition: Tube Feeding and TPN

Whenever I see a patient hooked up to some feeding system in a hospital drama on the TV, I cringe and hold my breath. I have yet to see a good representation of artificial nutrition on TV or in movies—many instances have been either totally medically incorrect or bordering on some kind of torture.

The decision to start artificial nutrition is not one any physician or dietitian takes lightly. We know it is a serious change in a person's lifestyle and may require further medical interventions and consistent management if set to be a long-term requirement.

Many patients and family members of patients I've come across have believed that IV fluids and artificial nutrition are the same thing, so just to clear some things up, artificial nutrition is not the same as artificial hydration. However, artificial hydration is part of a complete regimen for artificial nutrition. The most common form of artificial hydration is intravenous (IV) fluids.[46]

IV fluids are a mainstay of acute medical treatment, are temporary, and are very easily stopped. IV fluids are usually stopped several days before a patient is discharged, since most people recover well enough to be able to eat and drink enough for proper hydration and nutrition before discharge.

On the other hand, artificial nutrition uses fluids that have

---

45 Donna C. Tippett, "Dysphagia: What Happens During a Bedside Swallow Exam," Johns Hopkins Medicine, accessed February 20, 2022, https://www.hopkinsmedicine.org/health/treatment-tests-and-therapies/dysphagia-what-happens-during-a-bedside-swallow-exam.
46 "IV Fluids," Cleveland Clinic, accessed updated August 3, 2021, https://my.clevelandclinic.org/health/treatments/21635-iv-fluids.

water, calories, vitamins, minerals, and fat to replace food stuffs that someone would usually eat and drink. There are several formulations of the fluids used for artificial nutrition that are specific to distinctive disease processes, nutritional needs, and fluid requirements.

Artificial nutrition is achieved two ways: The first is via the gastrointestinal tract using liquid food. This is known as enteral feeding. Popular culture refers to enteral feeding as tube feeding. The second way bypasses the gastrointestinal tract all together and is given intravenously in a nutritionally dense fluid called total parenteral nutrition (TPN). **Each feeding mechanisms comes with its own risk and benefits, and both of them require different types of access into the body.**

The first way that enteral feeding is achieved is by placing a tube that starts in either the mouth or nose then goes down the esophagus and finally into the stomach, respectively called an orogastric (OG) or nasogastric (NG) tube. OG/NG tubes are great for temporary enteral feeding, but if more permanent enteral feeding is required, then a procedure is done to place a tube directly through the skin and into the stomach or small intestine. Many different surgical and medical considerations determine how and when that procedure is done, so I will not go into the specifics.[47]

TPN is a unique type of IV fluid because it's not safe to administer the fluid through the smaller IV line that patients usually have in their hands and arms, so it must be given by placing an IV line in one of the major veins of the body. Someone who might need TPN would be a patient who has some kind of structural problem that does not allow them to use their GI tract at all or whose significant dysfunction of the GI tract doesn't allow for full

---

47 Megan Dix, "Enteral Feeding: How It Works and When It's Used," Healthline, updated October 30, 2018, https://www.healthline.com/health/enteral-feeding.

absorption of nutrients.

Again, the decision to use TPN is not taken lightly, especially because there are some medical risks are associated with TPN use and because regular blood draws are necessary to ensure that the custom-made fluid meets the patient's nutritional needs.

When I was a resident, one of my favorite attending physicians told me, "Never plan to start TPN unless you have a plan to stop TPN." I still say this quote to myself every time I consider ordering it.

> **PRO TIP FOR DIET:** If you adhere to a specific dietary lifestyle (e.g., vegan), be sure to let your care team know so that you can be accommodated.

Commonly Prescribed Diets
1. Diabetic: Low sugar, consistent ratio of protein, fat, and carbohydrates with each meal
2. Cardiac: Low fat, low sodium: +/- a daily fluid limitation
3. Renal: Low potassium, low sodium: +/- a daily fluid limitation

Commonly Prescribed Food Textures
Regular: Any food texture that you desire (e.g., a whole apple)
Chopped: Food that is cut into bite-size pieces that can be immediately chewed by biting/tearing (e.g., apple cut into small pieces)
Soft: Moist foods that are easily swallowed (e.g., cooked apple)
Puréed: Finely ground or blended food (e.g., applesauce)

Commonly Prescribed Liquid Textures
Thin Liquids: (e.g., water)
Thickened Liquids: a tasteless starch is added to liquids to achieve the desired viscosity
• Honey Thick
• Nectar Thick
• Pudding Thick

Part Four: Day Two

Fact-Finding and Plan-Making

The first day of your hospitalization may have felt a bit hectic because you were going through basic testing and treatment to ensure your safety, to start some care, and to allow your hospitalist to start formulating a medical plan for you. However, day two may feel even busier because this is the day when your hospitalist will get more information about your condition that will allow them to set a more specific and longer-term care plan in action.

That's why day two is what I call the fact-finding and plan-making portion of your hospitalization. On day two, you're likely to undergo lab testing, get more radiologic studies, and possibly undergo procedures, all of which will give your doctors more information about your condition as well as your short- and long-term prognosis. You will also likely meet specialists who will be integral to your care.

Here in part four, we're going to focus on four areas:
1. *The types of clinical testing you are likely to encounter*
2. *How your social situation and your medical needs intersect*
3. *Healthcare Inequities*
4. *Some more helpful tips on how to get the most out of your clinical team*

Everything that happens on day two will be an important step in clarifying your diagnosis, creating a plan for your treatment, and addressing your subsequent longer-term recovery.

Clinical Testing

No one really likes tests, especially in the hospital, but they are central to getting a diagnosis and making an appropriate medical plan. Here are some of the ways you might undergo testing at the hospital:

- Labs: Blood Work & Other Body Fluids
- Radiology
- Functional Testing
- Endoscopic Tests
- Biopsies

A simple way to understand the purpose of various clinical tests is as follows: labs measure something, radiology takes a picture of something, functional tests observe how things are working, biopsies take a piece of something, and endoscopic tests let the doctors view something directly.

Labs: Blood Work

We're going to start with labs and blood work because most people are familiar with having to give blood or urine for a medical test.

The most common blood tests your hospitalist will order are a basic or complete metabolic panel (BMP or CMP) and a complete blood count (CBC). The BMP/CMP and CBC are fast ways for your physician to assess your electrolyte balance, see how well your kidneys and liver are working, and check to see if your body is showing signs of infection, inflammation, anemia, or other blood problems.[48]

Another common type of lab test is a culture, which is when the lab tests blood or any other body fluid for the presence of an infectious organism such as bacteria, fungi, or viruses. Cultures can take several days to show a definitive answer, so you may find those tests results are not available as quickly as others.[49]

> **REAL TALK:**
>
> **SEND-OUT TEST**
> When you hear your physician say, "This test is a send-out," they really mean that this test is not available at this hospital, so it must be sent to another facility. In most cases, the hospital you are admitted to will be able to complete all the testing needed, but there are some tests that require equipment or reagents that are only available at specific labs in your area.

Another commonly ordered test is called a PT/INR, which demonstrates how well your blood clots. There are several reasons this test might be ordered, including monitoring medication effects and liver function. Another important purpose of this test serves to ensure that you can safely have certain procedures done without excessive bleeding.

---

48 "Comprehensive Metabolic Panel (CMP)," Medline Plus, accessed February 20, 2022, https://medlineplus.gov/lab-tests/comprehensive-metabolic-panel-cmp/.
49 "Bacteria Culture Test," Medline Plus, accessed February 20, 2022, https://medlineplus.gov/lab-tests/bacteria-culture-test/.

To recap, here are some blood tests you may have regularly:

- **Complete blood count (CBC)**: measures how many red blood cells, white blood cells, and platelets are present in your blood[50]
- **Metabolic panel (BMP or CMP)**: measures electrolytes (e.g., sodium and potassium) and liver and kidney function[51]
- **International normalized ratio (INR)**: measures how well your blood is clotting[52]

Labs: Beyond Blood

Almost every body fluid can be collected for testing and can give important information about your health. Urine, stool, and sputum are regularly tested and tend to be relatively painless to give. Other body fluids that are in enclosed spaces, like cerebrospinal fluid (the fluid around your brain and spinal cord) or synovial fluid (the fluid around your joints), will require a small procedure to collect. You will be required to give permission for these procedures to be done. The paperwork you will sign to say, "Yes, I give permission for this to be done," is called an informed consent form.[53] Prior to signing an informed consent, the person carrying out the procedure will review the risks and benefits associated with the procedure and what, if anything, can be done instead of the

---

50 "Complete Blood Count," Mayo Health, December 22, 2020, https://www.mayoclinic.org/tests-procedures/complete-blood-count/about/pac-20384919.
51 "Comprehensive Metabolic Panel (CMP)," Medline Plus, accessed February 20, 2022, https://medlineplus.gov/lab-tests/comprehensive-metabolic-panel-cmp/.
52 "Prothrombin Time Test and INR (PT/INR)," Medline Plus, accessed February 20, 2022, https://medlineplus.gov/lab-tests/prothrombin-time-test-and-inr-ptinr/.
53 "Informed Consent—Adults," Medline Plus, accessed February 21, 2022, https://medlineplus.gov/ency/patientinstructions/000445.htm.

procedure—the alternatives. Feel free to ask questions, and be sure your concerns about pain and discomfort are addressed.

Radiology

Radiologists are physicians who specialize in assessing anatomy and function by interpreting all the various forms of imaging used to look into the body. There is a subset of radiologists called interventional radiologists, who have done additional training to learn how to do procedures with the guidance of various radiologic tools.[54]

Below are some of the most common forms of radiologic studies you will encounter in a hospitalization:

- Ultrasound (commonly called a sonograph)
- X-ray Imaging
- Computerized Tomography (commonly called CT or CAT scans)
- Magnetic Resonance Imaging (MRI)
- Nuclear Medicine

Ultrasounds

We're going to start small—*and* mighty.

The science behind ultrasound goes something like this: Sound waves are sent through the body via a small wand called a transducer. When the sound waves hit different tissues or fluids, they bounce back to the transducer, which then turns that information into a picture.

---

54   "What Is Interventional Radiology?," *Inside View* (blog), UVA Radiology and Medical Imaging, July 2, 2019, https://blog.radiology.virginia.edu/interventional-radiologist-definition/.

Most people are familiar with ultrasound in the setting of pregnancy, but ultrasound is used much more broadly than that—in fact, it can be used on almost any part of the body.

Ultrasounds provide a great deal of information very quickly, are quite portable, and are used for visualization during many procedures, making them a great tool for both diagnosis and treatment.

Beyond their versatility, ultrasounds are great because there is little risk involved with them, and many times ultrasounds can be done without having to move the patient around a great deal.[55]

X-ray Images

Because of how ubiquitous x-rays are, I wouldn't be surprised if most people have had at least one x-ray taken in their lifetime.

X-ray images are made by passing short wavelength electromagnetic particles (x-rays) through a defined portion of the body onto the machine. A picture is produced when the x-rays hit the machine at different speeds, after having passed through the body.[56] Air, fluid, and bone all look different in an x-ray—with bone looking bright white because it is the densest of the three, slowing down the x-rays the most.

Computerized Tomography: CT Scans

Physicians love computerized tomography because it creates incredibly detailed images in a very small amount of time. Because

---

[55] "Ultrasound," Mayo Clinic, March 17, 2020, https://www.mayoclinic.org/tests-procedures/ultrasound/about/pac-20395177.

[56] "X-Ray," Mayo Clinic, February 11, 2022, https://www.mayoclinic.org/tests-procedures/x-ray/about/pac-20395303.

of how fast CT scans can be done, they are really good for getting critical information in an emergency, which is why you will see CT scans ordered for trauma victims or people suspected of having a stroke or any other sudden and/or severe change in clinical status. CT scans are important tools in assessing the need for an emergency intervention. CT scans are also useful when determining the anatomy of unknown masses and can help find anatomic reasons for pain.

Physically, CT scan machines look like a big mechanical donut that you will lie flat in. CT uses x-rays and a computer to produce very detailed images. The donut shape of the machine is necessary because a CT machine rotates the x-rays around your body, taking pictures in slices so the computer can put them all together later.

You also may require something called contrast, depending on the reason for the CT. Think of contrast as a type of dye that adds further detail to the images produced, allowing the radiologist to see specific things not clearly visible otherwise.[57] Depending on the type of CT you are getting, you will either have to drink the contrast or it will be given in IV form.

Magnetic Resonance Imaging (MRI)

It's time to move one step up. If a CT scan is like a da Vinci painting, then you can think of the pictures produced by an MRI as a digital photo.

Getting an MRI is similar to getting a CT—contrast can be used, and you have to go into a big donut-like machine—but the hole that you go into is smaller, the sounds are louder, and the

---

57 "CT Scan," Mayo Clinic, January 6, 2022, https://www.mayoclinic.org/tests-procedures/ct-scan/about/pac-20393675.

test will take longer. Another difference is that MRI images are produced by pulses of radio frequency and a powerful magnetic field rather than the x-rays used in CT images. MRI is very good for giving details about soft tissues, organs, blood vessels, and joints.

Because MRI works with magnetic fields, it is important to keep metals that are unsafe out of the MRI machine. Though there are some medical implants that are safe for an MRI, there are others that are totally unsafe to be in the MRI machine. Each radiology department has their own protocols to ensure you can safely undergo an MRI, so you may be asked to fill out a questionnaire or furnish them other forms of information if needed.

REAL TALK:

CLAUSTROPHOBIA AND MRIS

It is not uncommon for people to be scared or uncomfortable when undergoing an MRI, given the small space that you have to lie in. However, canceling or aborting an MRI due to anxiety uses up precious resources and can prolong a hospitalization.

If you suffer from claustrophobia, please tell your physician at the first discussion of the need for an MRI. There are several medications for anxiety that can be used to help you keep calm and be more comfortable.

REAL TALK:

IMPLANTS/PROSTHESES

Do you have something implanted inside of you?

I know that sounds like a strange question, but hear me out. There are a ton of medical implants besides the cosmetic implants that usually come to mind, and your physicians need to know if you have any medical implants because they all serve important functions.

Things you might not even consider to be "implants" are implants. Any kind of pump in or on your body that's giving you medication should be considered an implant (e.g., baclofen pumps, insulin pumps). Pacemakers are implants. I also want you to consider any kind of artificial replacement for a body part (e.g., knee replacement) as an implant.

We need to know about pretty much *anything that wasn't originally a part of your body*, because that information will make a difference in what type of diagnosis we are looking for, what types of tests you can get, and even what type of medicines you need. Chances are, we'll be able to see if you have something like a pacemaker during a physical examination or on x-ray, but you shouldn't assume every implant is easily found.

Dr. Pieh's Mental Health Corner

UNDERSTANDING INFORMED CONSENT & HOW TO DEAL WITH ANXIETY AROUND TESTING

Feeling anxious or nervous about an upcoming test/procedure while in the hospital is common. Whenever an invasive test/procedure is to be performed, the treatment team must obtain informed consent from you to do the test/procedure. Informed consent requires the patient to be told what the procedure is, why it is needed at this time, what the risks and benefits are of the test/procedure, and any alternatives to the test/procedure.

Often, anxiety occurs when someone does not understand why the test is needed or when they are worried about it causing pain or discomfort. Ask your treatment team to discuss any concerns so that your team can answer any questions you may have. Furthermore, notify the treatment team if you are feeling anxious or nervous.

The following are some important questions to discuss with your treatment team when you are feeling nervous:

- What is the test/procedure?
- Why am I having this test/procedure?
- What happens if I don't get the test/procedure?
- What should I anticipate with this test/procedure? How long will it take?

After being informed, if you are still feeling anxious, try relaxation techniques such as mindfulness meditation.

> There are times when medication may be needed to help you feel less anxious so that the test or procedure can be performed. If you have tried relaxation techniques and are still feeling anxious, ask the treatment team if it is safe to be given medication for anxiety. If you are anxious about pain related to the test or procedure, ask if there are medications that can be given to address the pain.

Nuclear Medicine

This kind of radiology uses radioactively tagged material. I know *radioactive* and *nuclear* are alarming words, but the truth is that radiation and radioactive material are used quite frequently in medicine and in lots of different ways. Thus, physicians try to avoid frequent exposure by limiting the number of tests you get.

In nuclear medicine, radio-labeled material (a substance that has been combined with a tiny bit of radioactivity) is used to produce pictures of the anatomy and/or the function of an organ or mass. For instance, positron emission tomography (PET) is a test that can tell how a cancer is progressing so that the next steps in the treatment can be planned.[58]

Another type of test commonly used in nuclear medicine is a nuclear stress test. This test allows the radiologist to see how the heart functions under stress and determine if there is a possible atherosclerotic blockage of the heart's blood vessels.[59]

---

58 "Positron Emission Tomography Scan," Mayo Clinic, August 10, 2021, https://www.mayoclinic.org/tests-procedures/pet-scan/about/pac-20385078.
59 Richard Fogoros, "What Is a Nuclear Stress Test?," Medline Plus, updated January 14, 2022, https://www.verywellhealth.com/nuclear-stress-test-overview-4172096.

Functional Testing

Functional tests are kind of what they sound like. Your physician will be testing how well an organ is, well, functioning.

As I've mentioned, one way we test how well an organ is functioning is through blood work—things like measuring creatinine levels to see how well your kidneys are working or checking your red blood cells to see the health of your bone marrow—but some organs can be tested by taking real-time measurements. We can measure functions like how much blood is pumped by the heart (cardiac ECHO) or how long it takes your stomach to empty out the food you eat (gastric emptying test). Such tests can take place in the radiology or nuclear medicine suites, or even at bedside.

One of the more common functional tests done at the bedside is an electrocardiograph (ECG or EKG). This test measures and then illustrates the way that the heart's electrical current is working to create a heartbeat; if it's sending out electricity in an abnormal way, that could translate to the heart beating either too fast or too slow. Or if the heart is under stress from blocked coronary arteries, the pattern on the ECG will change in specific ways to show where the damage is occurring. Essentially, changes in the waves of the ECG clearly tell the doctors what is happening to your heart and how the heart's electrical currents are working.[60]

But those are just a few examples. There are so many other fantastic functional tests. For instance, we can measure how well the gallbladder is working through a hepatobiliary iminodiacetic

---

60 "What Is an Electrocardiogram?," Johns Hopkins Medicine, accessed February 21, 2022, https://www.hopkinsmedicine.org/health/treatment-tests-and-therapies/electrocardiogram.

acid (HIDA) scan; we can measure how well your lungs are breathing through pulmonary function tests (PFTs); and we can see the pattern of your brain waves with an electroencephalogram (EEG).[61]

For a functional test, you may find that you have to participate in some way. Eating may be restricted, or you may have to give a little bit of physical effort.

There are also some functional tests that do not take place in the hospital. If you're in need of one, your hospitalist may suggest you get one after you are discharged. An example of this is a pulmonary function test (PFT).

When someone who comes into the hospital can't breathe, we know it is *not* the time for us to do PFTs: It may be too difficult for them to withstand it, and the test will not tell us what their lungs look like at their baseline. The test will need to be done when they are feeling better.

Biopsies

In medicine, there is a saying: "Tissue is the issue." What that really means is that when there is an unknown mass in the body, we can't really make a plan for treatment until we identify the tissue—the issue.

There are some ways to attempt diagnosis without taking a piece of a mass, such as blood work or radiology. For instance, radiology can show us how the mass is situated, while blood work can describe what the mass is doing systemically to your body. But often times, a biopsy is the best and only way to know exactly

---

[61] "What Is Nuclear Medicine?," Mary Lanning Healthcare, accessed February 21, 2022, https://www.marylanning.org/our-services/imagingradiology/procedures/nuclear-medicine.

what the diagnosis is. As my pathology professor would always say, "Nothing hides from a microscope."

There are many ways to obtain a biopsy. During an acute hospitalization, if a biopsy is needed, the most common ways it will be done are either surgically (open biopsy), through minimally invasive methods by an interventional radiologist (IR-guided), or via an endoscopic exam.

An open biopsy is a surgical procedure where the surgeon opens the body and cuts off a part of the mass,[62] which is then tested immediately. Additional benefits to open biopsies include the possibility that the surgeon may be able to remove the entire mass, or that nearby lymph nodes can be removed to find out whether a potential cancer has spread, which is very important for how we determine the stage of a cancer.

An IR-guided biopsy, on the other hand, is a little different. In the case of these types of biopsies, the interventional radiologist will use some form of imaging to visualize both the mass and their instruments in real time as a small sample of the mass is taken through very small incisions. An example of this method would be employing ultrasound for a fine needle aspiration of a mass in the breast.[63]

Endoscopic Tests

I'm going to leave this portion on the broad side because there are enough types of endoscopic tests (e.g., colonoscopies, hysteroscopies) to make up an entirely new book. What I will say is that endoscopic testing essentially encompasses a flexible tube with a

---

62   "Biopsies—Overview," RadiologyInfo.org, February 20, 2019, https://www.radiologyinfo.org/en/info/biopgen.
63   "Biopsies—Overview," RadiologyInfo.org.

light and camera being inserted into the body to take pictures, take biopsies, and enact procedures.[64]

> **REAL TALK:**
>
> **HOSPITALIZATION MIGHT OVERRIDE PREVIOUSLY SCHEDULED TESTS**
>
> "If I'm already hospitalized, why can't I get a test I was already scheduled for?"
>
> I get this question a lot. For example, imagine a patient who is in the hospital because they have pneumonia, *and* they have an appointment scheduled for an MRI of their knee the following week. Despite their requests, it is unlikely that they will get that MRI during their current hospitalization for a few reasons:
>
> - We must prioritize the treatments that are necessary for the patient's acute care. After all, that outcome is the focus of the hospitalization.
> - Not every test, specialist, and/or procedure is available in every hospital.
> - Insurance can designate certain treatments as inpatient versus outpatient for coverage purposes, so the treatment or medication may not qualify to be done during a hospitalization.

---

64 "Types of Endoscopy," Cancer.net, June 2019, https://www.cancer.net/navigating-cancer-care/diagnosing-cancer/tests-and-procedures/types-endoscopy.

PRO TIP FOR TESTING IN THE HOSPITAL: When you are discussing tests with your hospitalist, you should be armed with a written list of questions. If you're not sure what to ask, here are a few questions to get you started:

1. What information am I going to get out of this?
2. Is this test/procedure also a treatment, or is this purely for diagnosis?
3. What are the risks associated with the test/procedure?
4. Are there any feasible alternatives to this test/procedure?
5. What will the next steps be after I get this done?
6. What can be done to help make me comfortable during the test/procedure?

Social Issues

I always tell my patients that planning for a safe discharge begins on day one of their admission.

Your hospitalist and care team are always thinking about how you will be cared for after you are discharged. This means they will be working on a way for you to receive care after you leave, and they are also finding the next safe place for you to go if you cannot go home. Oftentimes, that determination is affected by your social situation—what I will define as your ability to obtain and maintain safe housing, food, and physical security. The reasons that your social situation may be compromised can come down to everything from family dynamics to financial situations to insurance.

Your hospitalist cannot navigate your social needs by themselves. With a plethora of insurance plans and their ever-changing rules, in addition to numerous community resources available, coordinating your care after discharge requires a team approach. The social worker and the case manager are going to be the key players in your care team to help you navigate your medical needs and social situation in order to ensure a safe and smooth transition out of the hospital.

Get ready to take some notes because knowing how to utilize the people who will help coordinate services to fit your specific situation is crucial to your success in staying out of the hospital after discharge.

Social Workers

We'll start with the social worker because most people have a general idea of who social workers are. That familiarity is probably due to the fact that they aren't unique to the hospital; as you may already know, they work in many different areas and help all kinds of people navigate tough social problems.

To be clear, although there are social workers in the hospital, a social worker is not a nurse. They usually aren't medically trained, although they may have some very specific medical knowledge, if needed, to work with special populations.

The hospital-based social worker helps people navigate all the social problems that can complicate life in and out of the hospital, such as food and housing insecurities. Victims of domestic violence can use the hospital social worker to find safe housing and other needed services.

Another focus of the social worker is to help patients locate psychiatric supports outside of the hospital. On a similar note, if someone is entangled in the court system in some way, their own social worker may follow them in the hospital if necessary. We often see that situation with children who are in custody of the state. A social worker may also be of use in cases with elderly patients, where we sometimes see patterns of unsafe housing, in addition to dementia, hoarding, food insecurity, and loneliness.

The above examples are just a few of the many ways that social workers can be of aid in the hospital. They really are an excellent resource, so I highly suggest you take advantage of their services.[65]

---

65 "What Do Medical Social Workers Do?," USC Suzanne Dworak-Peck School of Social Work, July 13, 2018, https://dworakpeck.usc.edu/news/what-do-medical-social-workers-do.

Case Manager

Distinct from the social worker is the case manager (some hospitals may use the term *case workers*). I imagine they're a bit elusive to the average Joe because they're more specific to the medical world. Let's clear that right up!

Think of a case manager as a cross between a nurse and a social worker. This person's job is to understand how to coordinate the care you will need after discharge, which can be complicated due to your specific social situation, health insurance, and community resources. Case managers use their knowledge of post–acute care facilities, insurance qualifications, and other resources available to create a plan for your specific medical needs, ensuring your success after discharge.

Unlike a social worker, a case manager is likely to be nurse too. Here are some of the ways a case manager can help you navigate your hospitalization and prepare for discharge:

- To clarify your concerns about discharge to your clinical care team
- To determine insurance technicalities that may complicate or limit your choices after discharge
- To understand post-hospitalization care (e.g., long-term antibiotics, wound care, necessary appointments with a specialist)
- To find a safe place for you to go after the hospital if you can't go home
- To find the best place for end-of-life care (e.g., at home, a hospice house, or a skilled nursing facility)[66]

---

[66] Elizabeth Davis, "Duties and Types of Case Managers," Verywell Health, updated November 11, 2020, https://www.verywellhealth.com/what-does-a-case-manager-do-1738560.

Let's pretend you have a wound that needs to be cared for after you leave the hospital. Your case manager will be able to understand the daily notes and wound care orders in your chart, other issues complicating your condition, what your specialists are saying, what your insurance covers, and ultimately what kind of medical care the wound will require after you leave the hospital. The case manager will assess how feasible it is to care for that wound at home, or if the wound needs complex care, the case manager may arrange a temporary stay at a facility that can do the necessary care.

The beauty of a case manager comes from having somebody who understands the intersection between social and medical needs, because not all care takes place in the hospital. The case manager's role truly cannot be replicated.

> **PRO TIPS FOR TALKING TO CASE MANAGERS**
> - Make sure you find out who your case manager for the day is because it can change on a regular basis!
> - Tell the case manager about your transportation needs if you have trouble getting to your outpatient appointments.
> - Be open and honest about limitations to care for yourself or a loved one at home.
> - Don't put on a brave face for your case manager. They need to know how you're really doing so that they can plug you into other resources, if need be.

Questions to Ask Yourself Before Meeting with Your Case Manager or Social Worker

I want you to ask yourself these questions before meeting with your case manager or social worker because the answers will help guide you to what you need make a safe discharge plan.

1. **Where do I want to go after I leave the hospital?**

Most people want to go home after the hospital, but that's not always possible. So, if home isn't the next place for you or your loved one, what are other options? Places like rehabilitation centers and nursing homes that can deliver short- or long-term care are referred to as post–acute care facilities. It's normal for people to have certain preferences when discussing post–acute care facilities—like wanting to be placed near family or going to a facility they're already familiar with. So, consider where you would like to continue your care and rehabilitation prior to going home. If home is a feasible option and your first preference, please let your social worker and case manager know.

2. **What social and emotional supports do I have while I am in the hospital and when I leave the hospital?**

Social and emotional supports are very important for all of your medical needs. You're not going to get better if you don't feel supported, and there's research to back that up; for instance, one study found that wounds heal more slowly in mice that were socially isolated.[67]

---

67 Leah M. Pyter et al., "The Effects of Social Isolation on Wound Healing Mechanisms in Mice," *Physiology & Behavior* 127 (2014): 64–70, https://doi.org/10.1016/j.physbeh.2014.01.008.

Feeling socially and emotionally supported is just as important as any prescription, so be honest with your social worker or case manager about how you suspect you'll be feeling after you leave the hospital and who in your life will be able to help you. If you will be alone and feel as if you need assistance with your medical needs or to do the daily activities of your life, your case manager can request services like a visiting nurse, plug you into resources like Meals on Wheels, or help you start the process of getting assistance in your home with a personal care attendant. You also could say the exact opposite—that you'll be living with the best family members in the world and will be greatly supported—and that's fine too. In that case, your case manager will make sure you all have the necessary equipment and medication to guarantee you can safely continue convalescing at home.

3. **What type of care am I safely willing and able to do for myself/my loved one? What will I need help with when I leave the hospital to ensure that all my/their needs are met?**

I want to spend a little extra time on this question (i.e., *What do I need help with?*) because it's a big one, and I want everyone to be very honest with themselves when it comes to answering it.

I know of a person who got sick in his 40s from cancer. After it became clear that there were no more curative treatments and that he was dying, he left the hospital to go home with hospice—where his family was to attend to him during his final days. That arrangement usually works out fine, but in this case, his medical needs were past his family's ability to care for him.

His family tried their best, but in the end, they all felt that he suffered greatly—which left them feeling horrible about themselves, in addition to the grief of losing someone they loved. After many discussions with them, I learned that the people responsible for most of his care felt that some of it was above their abilities, but they felt they had to keep doing it because he requested to die at home. They never told the case manager at the hospital nor the hospice nurses how out of their element they felt. In hindsight, this gentleman and his family may have had a better experience if there had been more support from trained nursing staff 24/7 in his home or if he even spent some more time in the hospital having his pain addressed more aggressively prior to going home with hospice.

This person's case is not unlike others that I see. When a patient's needs are greater than the abilities of those charged with caring for them at home, they end up suffering in silence or with repeated hospitalizations when caregivers feel in crisis. This recurrence leaves everyone involved feeling like failures, and it increases the chance that something unwanted will happen. I have seen it happen over and over again.

Overall, these questions are so important because they get at the heart of what makes a safe discharge plan: having a safe place, consistent resources, and good supports to continue getting care. I highly recommend you go through these thoroughly so that you can be prepared to have an honest conversation with your case manager and social worker.

Healthcare Inequity

In 2016, a study detailed the many false beliefs that White medical students held about Black patients, specifically with 73% endorsing at least one false belief—one of them being that Black patients have a higher tolerance for pain than White patients.[68] For transgender patients, one in three reported having to teach their doctors about their identity in order to get proper care, while 15% of LGBTQ+ patients described avoiding or postponing medical treatment due to discrimination.[69] For patients with disabilities, one study reported that only 52% of patients received a referral to a specialist for an organ transplant evaluation when it was medically appropriate.[70] Moreover, female pain has been minimized as hysteria throughout history, and today, women are less likely than men to have their pain adequately addressed by healthcare providers.[71] While you would be hard-pressed to find a single healthcare provider who would openly admit to treating patients differently based on their race, accent, disability, gender, identity, or sexual orientation, the disparate healthcare outcomes of these groups

---

68   Kelly M. Hoffman et al., "Racial Bias in Pain Assessment and Treatment Recommendations, and False Beliefs About Biological Differences Between Blacks and Whites," *PNAS* 113, no. 16 (2016): 4296–4301, https://doi.org/10.1073/pnas.1516047113.
69   Sharita Gruberg, Lindsay Mahowald, and John Halpin, "The State of the LGBTQ Community in 2020," Center for American Progress (CAP), October 6, 2020, https://www.americanprogress.org/issues/lgbtq-rights/reports/2020/10/06/491052/state-lgbtq-community-2020/.
70   Ari Ne'eman, Steven Kapp, and Caroline Narby, "Organ Transplantation and People with I/DD: A Review of Research, Policy and Next Steps," Autistic Self Advocacy Network, March 2013, https://autisticadvocacy.org/policy/briefs/organ-transplantation-and-people-with-idd-a-review-of-research-policy-and-next-steps/.
71   Esther H. Chen et al., "Gender Disparity in Analgesic Treatment of Emergency Department Patients with Acute Abdominal Pain," *Academic Emergency Medicine* 15, no. 5 (2008): 414–418, https://pubmed.ncbi.nlm.nih.gov/18439195/.

tells a different story. Unfortunately, we have evidence that people will receive different care and thus have different experiences and outcomes based on who they are.

Systemic discrimination has been built into and continues to be a shameful feature of our healthcare system. For some readers, this may come as shocking news, but for others of you, I know you are already aware of the way implicit and explicit biases play out in healthcare.

For instance, one of my Black female patients felt like her pain was not being treated appropriately, and whenever she received her medication, she would tell the nurse, "These are not working."

The nurse would reply, "You're not due for more pain medications for another six hours."

When I got the report from the nurse, she told me, "This lady just keeps asking for more pain meds. She just wants more no matter what."

When I sat down to talk to my patient, she was very distraught and still in a lot of pain. She explained, "The nurse wasn't really listening. I wasn't asking for *more* pain medication; I was asking for my pain to be addressed differently. I was trying to tell her that the pain medication *wasn't* working at all."

After our conversation, my patient and I sat down and went over a list of pain medications she had tried. We found a pattern that indicated opiates didn't work well for her, so we started her on alternatives as soon as we could, and her pain eventually improved.

Later on, my patient called out how she felt discriminated against in this situation. She said, "Because I'm a Black woman, they think I'm being dramatic or I want something I shouldn't get, and they don't want to listen to what I'm saying."

This is one real-life example of the statistics I've shared with you.

This patient tried to advocate for herself and sought out help to get her message across. When she felt unheard she called her primary care physician, who in-turn reached out to me directly and alerted me about the patient's pain and concerns of discrimination.

Feel free to lean on your support system for people who can help you navigate your hospitalization, explain things, speak directly to your care team, and be an additional advocate—which includes any external help (e.g., your primary care doctor, family members who may be medically savvy, or spiritual leaders).

One resource that exists within the hospital is the patient advocacy (may also be called patient relations) department. The goal of a patient advocate is to provide a space for patients to be heard and to communicate their concerns, helping them navigate and resolve problems with their care. Though a patient advocate is a representative of the hospital, they have a responsibility to be a champion for patients as well. A patient advocate can help you understand where you're getting stuck and may have some insights into the way the hospital works. Additionally, they have access to hospital leadership, so they can escalate your issue more directly.[72]

Note: I am not suggesting that working with a patient advocate will make healthcare disparities disappear. It's just one avenue for you to advocate for yourself I want you to be aware of.

Addressing Healthcare Inequity and Disparities: What Is Being Done

Some years ago, a group of medical students started questioning why there is a race-based component in the equation for glomerular filtration rate (eGFR)— which determines how well your

---

[72] Health Net Federal Services, "Hospital Patient Advocates," www.hnfs.com, accessed June 11, 2022, https://www.hnfs.com/content/hnfs/home/tw/bene/res/hospital-stay/patient_advocates.html.

kidneys are working. These tenacious young minds did not let up when given the usual answers by their teachers. Because of their rightful questioning a movement was started to re-consider the use of race in the calculation of kidney function. In 2021, the American Society of Nephrologists got together and decided that race-based estimations for eGFR should no longer be used.[73]

I know this case doesn't sound like a big deal, but it's a *huge* deal in medicine. The eGFR is based on a mathematical equation that has been around for decades, and the color of the patient's skin was just a part of the equation. The eGFR determines the severity of your kidney disease, and thus treatment decisions are made based on that calculation, which meant that people whom nephrologists perceived as Black were treated differently because bias was built into the math. If you stop and think about it for a minute, the whole thing just doesn't make sense. How can a mathematical equation change based on someone else's perception of what your race is? Does your kidney know how dark your skin is or how straight your hair is? What category do recipients of a kidney transplant fall into if the donor is of a different race?

Clearly, this part of the equation didn't make sense, but we've been treating patients based on its results for decades. So, when the nephrologists got together and decided to do without the race-based part of the equation, it was really big news—specifically because it's going to change a ton of care and outcomes for people.

The problem now lies with changing the systems that have been built around this equation. Across the nation and world, computer systems in labs have that outdated equation built into them. Furthermore, nephrologists who have been practicing for

---

[73] Cynthia Delgado et al., "A Unifying Approach for GFR Estimation," *Journal of the American Society of Nephrology* 32, no. 12 (2021): 2994–3015, https://doi.org/10.1681/ASN.2021070988.

many years now have to unlearn what they had accepted. Medical students will also have to be trained in a new way, medical records will have to be changed, and so on.

Those issues encompass the problem that we are up against when addressing healthcare inequities and disparities. It's a system-wide problem that starts with the education of medical and nursing students, and then continues on to their practices and the system built to support and advance those practices.

There are efforts all over the nation aimed at how we educate, recruit, retain, and support healthcare providers to deliver on the promise of medicine. It is my hope that the next generation of physicians and nurses continues to improve on the system so that one day we can rid ourselves of healthcare inequities and disparities.

Tips from Your Hospitalist

When you're in the hospital, it's natural to feel confused, scared, and lost. Your care team can support you through these emotions, and with some effort on your part, you can gain some confidence and feel more in control through the entire process.

Here are a few more suggestions to help you get the information you need and be the driver of your care:

- Keep a written list of daily questions.
- Identify one person with whom your provider should communicate for your care.
- Get the name and business card of every physician on your care team (including specialists).
- Be open and honest about your abilities, social and medical support, and any other concerns.
- Be realistic about your goals.
- Keep your support system updated about what you will need when you leave the hospital.

Always, always, always keep a pen and paper by the bedside table to *write down your questions* as they come to you. We've all had the feeling of forgetting what you wanted to ask the doctor the second they walk into the room. This forgetfulness usually happens because the running list of questions in your head is instantaneously replaced by *who is this person again?* Then, before you have a chance to think, the physician will say, "How are you feeling today?" To which most of us instinctively say, "I'm fine," because it's immediate and involuntary—even if you were just having diarrhea, your knee hurts, or your plans for staying with your sister just fell through and you no longer have a place to go after discharge.

My point is get that piece of paper and pen so that you have your questions handy, even if you have to ask your nurse for a piece of paper out of the printer.

I want to be clear that it's not your fault if you forget what your question was—it's just what happens when there are a lot of moving pieces and too many different names and faces. In a hospital, changes come very quickly, and to top it all off, you just don't feel well. So, those are the exact reasons why writing down your questions as they come is a useful tactic. The goal is to make sure you're able to communicate what you need.

This following tip is an important one: *Identify a care partner and the person with whom your providers should communicate.* Your care partner is the person in your social support network who is going to help you during and after your hospitalization. To streamline communications and to keep things consistent, your care partner should be the only person who is speaking to your care team, in addition to yourself. For most people, their care partner tends to be the same person they have identified as their healthcare proxy, whether or not that person is actively making decisions for them. If you are able to make your own medical decisions and are comfortable disseminating information to your family, it will be assumed that you can do so, and your hospitalist may not know that you expected them to call your care partner. If you want regular updates given to your care partner or anyone else, clearly make that request known.

It is not a reasonable expectation that your hospitalist will be able to call multiple family members to give multiple updates daily. Instead, you should expect that your hospitalist will be able to give one update to your care partner on a regular basis—excluding if there is a critical change in your care that would require multiple discussions in one day—and that person will be the one to share the information with others according to your wishes.

Another tactic that will help you stay organized in the hospital is to *get the name and business card of every physician on your care team*, including specialists. If you get the name and business card of every physician whom you see, you will know who is playing what role in your care and be able to correlate that information with the care plan after discharge.

I really want to encourage you to *be open and honest with your team about your ability to care for yourself, what your social situation is, and any other health concerns or fears you have*, even if you don't think they have anything to do with your current hospitalization.

Being open and honest with your hospitalist strengthens the therapeutic relationship and helps give a more complete picture of who you are as well as a better understanding of how to best treat you.

You may even highlight something your providers weren't aware of that was complicating your care. For example, I had a patient who had a run of hospitalizations for uncontrolled heart failure symptoms. He was known to be inconsistent with his medications, so at the time that I did his admission, I, too, did what all the previous hospitalists did for him to treat his heart failure: restart his medications, specifically a class of medications called diuretics, which help you to produce urine and expel excess fluid from the body.

A few hours after he was hospitalized, his nurse called me and said, "The patient told me why he's constantly having heart failure and not taking his medication."

"Why?" I asked, puzzled, expecting to hear that he wasn't able to get the medications from his pharmacy or didn't like a side effect.

It turned out that his foreskin was closing over the tip of his penis—making urination difficult and painful, which made it hard for him to tolerate taking the diuretics he was prescribed. He stopped taking his heart medication so he could avoid painful urination. In the end, what he really needed was a circumcision, after which he could comfortably take his diuretics and keep his heart failure symptoms under control. I never would have consulted a urologist for a circumcision if he had not spoken up and revealed his true concern to his nurse.

Next, try to *be realistic about your goals*.

Being realistic is sometimes the hardest thing to do. Every doctor who treats elderly patients in the hospital can tell you a similar story: The family of a patient who is admitted for worsening confusion will say, "My mother was an airline pilot," or, "My father was a physicist," and then expect that their parent's functional and mental status will be able to return to something close to their highest level of function.

When this happens to me, the next question I like to ask is "When was the last time that Mom/Dad was able to function like that?"

Often, I find out that they haven't been at that level for many years. It is only natural that we always see our parents and grandparents as the bright and vibrant people we remember, so it's hard to see and accept declines in the people we love.

To be fair, sometimes it goes the other way. I once had a patient tell me their grandmother was a professional ballroom dancer. After some skepticism on my end, he showed me a video of her ballroom dancing three days before she was hospitalized.

That information helped me understand what her functional status was, and within a number of days, she was back to her bright and joyous self. A few weeks later, he called the office to tell me that she was once again dancing. In this case, her grandson had a clear example of what her baseline was and used it to communicate a realistic goal for her.

The unfortunate truth is that those who have chronic and/or progressive diseases are the people who tend to visit hospitals frequently, and an acute hospitalization is unlikely to totally cure their illness. The best that may be achievable is to get them back to a level of function or comfort that allows them to continue managing their chronic illness.

Sometimes it's hard to hear and accept that getting totally better isn't possible. We get it. It's our job to help walk you through the process of figuring out what is and isn't possible. It might feel morbid to bring death up here too, but there are going to be times when the most realistic and appropriate thing we can do is to acknowledge that continuing with aggressive treatments will not change the outcome of a terminal illness, and we must change our care plan from that of intervention to one that ensures comfort at the end of life.

The final thing I recommend that you do is *keep your support system updated about what you will need when you leave the hospital.* Make sure that your family and friends can help you with any appointments, medications, and/or special equipment you may need, because those things will be key in getting you well and keeping you out of the hospital.

Dr. Pieh's Mental Health Corner

VISUALIZATION AND RELAXATION TECHNIQUES

Visualization is the process of creating images in your mind that allow your mind and body to relax. It can help with managing stress, anxiety, and depression and reducing pain, and in some cases, it can also help lower blood pressure, lessen nausea, and give you a better overall sense of control and well-being. Guided imagery is one visualization technique that only requires you to find a quiet and comfortable spot where you can be alone for 15 minutes.

To do guided imagery, follow these steps:

1. Sit or lie down in a quiet place that is also comfortable (bed, couch, yoga mat, or chair).
2. Close your eyes.
3. Take several deep breaths. Inhale and exhale deeply. You will keep breathing deeply as you continue throughout this relaxation technique.
4. Imagine a peaceful and pleasant scene or image (e.g., quiet beach, peaceful garden, lush forest, majestic mountain range), or think of a favorite place in nature that makes you relax.
5. Think of all the details of that scene. Notice the sounds, images, and scents—think about what you see, what you hear, what you smell, and what you might feel. Include all of the details that make this place peaceful or calming.
6. Envision yourself walking along a path, noticing the details and sounds as you walk.
7. After 15 minutes, count to three and open your eyes.

You can also access guided imagery on various app platforms and YouTube.

Another useful relaxation technique is square breathing,* a simple breathing technique that can be used to address feelings of worry, panic, and anxiety. It can help regulate your breathing and heart rate, alleviate stress, and promote relaxation. The goal is to take slow, deep breaths:

1. Breathe in for four counts.
2. Hold for four counts.
3. Breathe out for four counts.
4. Hold for four counts.

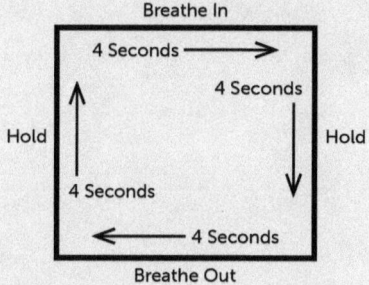

*If you have COPD or other respiratory concerns, please check with your primary team before trying this technique.

Part Five: Days Three and Four

Treatment

The overall themes of days three and four will be to continue receiving the necessary medications and therapies to treat your acute illness and to plan for what you will need after discharge. At this point, you were admitted to the hospital and stabilized, and you have completed a bunch of labs and other tests, all so your hospitalist was able to make a treatment plan for you.

Because your treatment will be specific to your case and can range from a variety of things—from new medications to surgery to various procedures—I won't speak directly about any regimens. The most important thing I can tell you about now is *how you can be an active participant in your care and, most importantly, easy steps to take that can help you avoid getting sicker.*

This knowledge will be the most valuable to you because it has the potential to expedite your recovery, keep you from getting common hospital ailments, like pneumonia, and get you out of the hospital sooner.

Ultimately, the objective of your hospitalization may vary based on your preferences (i.e., whatever *getting better* means to you), but an overarching goal for everyone tends to be not getting worse—which is why we will be discussing the following:

- Your hospitalization workout routine
- Keeping your spirits up
- Making your follow-up appointments early
- Seeing specialists

The advice I'm about to share is crucial because being in the hospital upturns your life: You're sleeping in a bed you're not used to, you're not really moving around, you're not eating the foods you normally eat, and you're not going to the bathroom the same way you did before.

All of this change in lifestyle exposes you to certain risks in the hospital—what we will call nosocomial complications. The most common nosocomial complications are infections, injuries from falls, and confusion—known as delirium—in the setting of acute illness and hospitalization. All of these nosocomial complications are associated with longer hospitalizations, worse outcomes, and a higher chance of death—which is why it's incredibly important that you take an active part in your own care and focus not only on the medical aspects of your care but also your mental health and emotional well-being.

Your Hospitalization Workout Routine

One of the best ways to avoid complication in the hospital is to become an active participant in your care. In this section, I've listed some ways you can do just that:

1. Get out of bed
2. Take deep breaths using your incentive spirometer
3. Do your physical, occupational, and speech therapy
4. Stick to your prescribed diet

First, *get out of bed.*

I know that sounds silly because you're in a hospital, where there are tons of people who can take care of you. You may also be in pain or discomfort that you feel is limiting your mobility, and all the while, your friends and family are likely telling you to get as much rest and relaxation in bed as you can.

But as the law of physics states, a body at rest will stay at rest, and a body in motion will stay in motion, so will you. As silly as it sounds, the longer you stay in bed, the longer you will stay in bed. That fact means you have to get moving, my friend. Getting up and out of the bed to go to the bathroom, eat your meals, walk the halls, or even to sit in a chair for a while are types of movements that will help you get stronger, avoid infection, avoid confusion, and prevent injury.

Hospital-associated deconditioning is the loss of function that occurs during an acute hospitalization. Hospital-associated deconditioning is due to a number of complex factors and affects each patient differently, so there is no guarantee that you can avoid it. However, getting up and moving around in a safe manner is one way you can thwart a bad case of deconditioning. So, get up, go to the bathroom, and ask your nurse where you're allowed to walk in the hospital. You may even be able to go for a little walk outside if possible.

Next, *take deep breaths using your incentive spirometer*. An incentive spirometer is a tool that encourages you to expand your lungs and take deeper breaths.[74] It looks like a small plastic box with a hose and mouthpiece attached. Your job will be to use the incentive spirometer as much as possible to help you take nice deep breaths. Again, this action may sound like a ridiculous task, but when you are stuck in bed, in pain, or feeling sick, trust me when I say that you are probably *not* taking as deep of breaths as usual. Taking deep breaths using the incentive spirometer is especially useful when it comes to preventing pneumonia in the hospital.

---

74 "Incentive Spirometry," Physiopedia, accessed February 21, 2022, https://www.physio-pedia.com/Incentive_Spirometry.

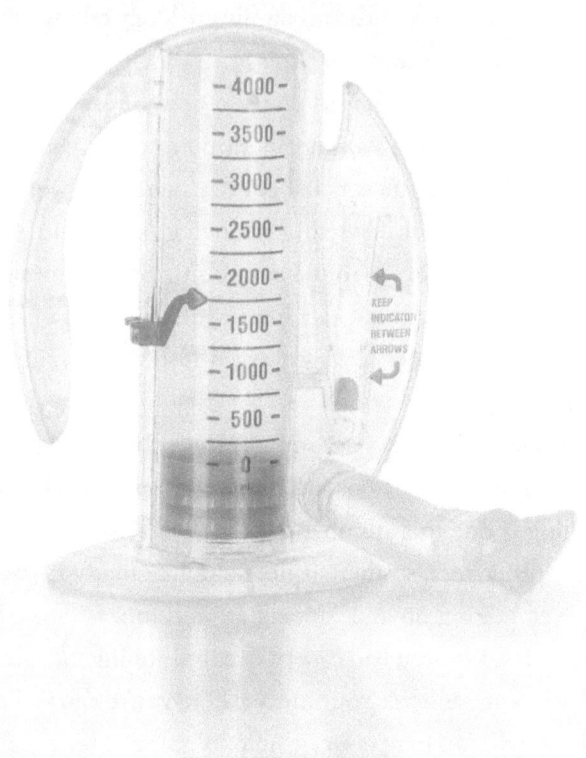

Example of an incentive spirometer.

The official prescription is usually 10 times an hour, during every hour that you're awake. That amount may sound overwhelming, but if you just do it while you're watching commercials on TV, you'll surpass the 10-breath mark without even realizing it.[75] If you or your loved one is not automatically given this device, please feel free to request one.

I believe in this tool so much that it is a must-have in my

---

75 "Incentive Spirometry," Physiopedia.

figurative "medical toolbox." In fact, I order them so often that a medical student who was once working with me would go straight to the supply room and grab one or two on each floor for our patients during rounds. Now *that* was a great student.

Another important step in participating in your care is to *do your physical therapy (PT), occupational therapy (OT), and/or speech therapy (ST)*. First, I want to discuss what your interactions with these therapists will be like, because your treatment may be different from what you're thinking.

The job of PT/OT/ST during an acute hospitalization is to assess your safety and make a care plan for any limitations with movement, eating, and communicating. For example, if you had a stroke that affected your speech and swallowing the speech pathologist in the hospital will focus on determining what types of food you can swallow safely to avoid choking, and also help you find a temporary solution, like using a small whiteboard, so that you can communicate during your hospitalization. The longer-term goal of improving speech and readdressing dietary changes as swallowing improves will be done with a speech pathologist you see on a regular basis in their office or in a post–acute care facility.

Similarly, an occupational therapist will assess a patient's safety when it comes to performing an action. They will be inspecting whether or not the person can safely use a toilet, for example, or put on socks. Depending on how the patient does, they may be furnished with equipment to help with these tasks.

Last, a physical therapist in the hospital will home in on how well a patient can move through space—for example, ascertaining whether the patient can get out of bed or move around their room. They will help the care team determine if the patient can safely return home after discharge or if additional rehabilitation services and/or equipment will be needed.[76]

Alternatively, on an outpatient basis, these types of therapists can spend more time with patients to relearn skills, get stronger, speak clearly, use new assistive devices, and so on. Learning how to write again after having a stroke, to walk with a new prosthetic, or to speak as they did before a traumatic injury are examples of what these therapies might involve outside of the hospital. That's where the patient will work with the hope of returning to their previous level of function—not during an acute hospitalization. In the hospital, PT, OT, and ST are really focused on helping achieve your acute needs, assessing your safety, and helping to make a plan for your continued therapy needs after discharge.

Because of these therapists' assessments, you might leave the hospital with new equipment, like a walker, crutches, or a shower chair. Please, please, please use this equipment. Treat your new equipment as a prescription, like any other medicine or therapy. Such things are necessary to keep you safe and avoid injury.

Additionally, you may be prescribed a new diet texture if your speech therapist believes you can't safely eat regular food. Their prescription is like any other prescription, necessary for your safety and part of your treatment plan.

Which leads me to my last piece of advice—*stick to your prescribed diet.*

I won't go too deep into this one because we've already gone over prescribed diets, but I do want to remind you of the importance of staying on these diets for as long as they are ordered. It may be a temporary change, or a more permanent one.

Food is important in the process of recovery and managing

---

[76] "OT vs. PT vs. SLP," OTPotential, accessed February 22, 2022, https://otpotential.com/occupationaltherapy-vs-physicaltherapy-vs-speechtherapy.

chronic illnesses. Changes to the texture of your solid foods and/or liquids may be necessary to ensure your safety by decreasing the chance that you aspirate or choke while eating. Prescribed limitations on salt, potassium, sugars, or fluids often go hand in hand with how well your prescription medications will work to help manage your symptoms. So, although your brother-in-law brought you your favorite cranberry-orange scone, if it is on the "no eat" list for any reason, please feel free to take a sniff, but try not to eat it.

Dr. Pich's Mental Health Corner

SLEEP

Getting sleep in the hospital can be difficult. Know what to expect if you should need to be hospitalized. There may be tests or other procedures that need to be done at specific times throughout the day or night.

- Turn off the TV, and turn off your phone when it is time to sleep. The light from the phone or TV can be activating and keep you awake.
- Try reading a book or magazine instead of watching TV—reading can also help to distract you if you are feeling anxious or nervous about an upcoming procedure.
- Make sure to have the lights on/shades up during the day and lights off/shades down at night.
- Ask to review your medications with your team if you suspect that a medication may be keeping you up; you

> - can ask to adjust the time the medication is given, as some medications can be given anytime.
> - If pain or discomfort is preventing you from being able to sleep, make sure to notify your treatment team.

If you have questions about how to continue your prescribed diet after discharge, you can ask to have a consult with the hospital nutritionist or dietitian. They will be able to give more education on why you need this prescribed diet and to help you find ways to follow it in your daily life. Be open about how you normally eat at home, your favorite foods, and cultural eating practices because all this affects how you are able to continue your diet at home.

Sticking to this new diet may be a lifetime practice, so be patient with yourself!

REAL TALK:

DON'T SKIP PT/OT/ST

There is no set time for when the PT/OT/ST come to see your in the hospital. If the therapist shows up when you are doing something else (i.e., eating lunch); stop what you are doing so you can work with them. If you ask the therapist to come back later, you may just miss out on the chance to be seen that day. Remember, the therapist's, assessments and treatment plans are a vital part of your daily care and discharge planning.

Dr. Pieh's Mental Health Corner

AVOIDING DELIRIUM

Delirium is an altered state of consciousness that can occur when someone is ill. Delirium can happen to anyone during their hospitalization, but those who already have an underlying brain disorder, such as dementia, are at most risk. Delirium can present with agitation, confusion, excessive fatigue, or periods of intermittent sedation. Severe cases of delirium can include hallucinations and paranoia. Delirium is not only associated with prolonged hospitalizations but also with higher rates of mortality.[77]

Here are some things you can do to help decrease the risk of developing delirium:

1. Try to keep a normal sleep-wake cycle where you are sleeping at night and awake and active (as possible) during the day.
2. If you find yourself feeling confused or disoriented, notify your treatment team.
3. Ask family or friends to keep an eye out for you behaving differently. Ask your family or support network to also keep track if you do not seem like yourself. They should notify the treatment team of their concerns.
4. Address uncontrolled pain, as it can increase your risk of delirium.

---

77 Esther Hereema, "Delirium: Higher Chance of Death and Increased Risk of Dementia," Verywell Health, updated January 27, 2020, https://www.verywell-health.com/delirium-higher-mortality-rate-and-risk-of-dementia-98840.

5. Be up-front about any regular or heavy alcohol use. If hospitalized, you may be at risk of developing confusion or delirium related to alcohol withdrawal.
6. Bring in pictures from family or friends to put around the room.
7. Ask the nurse to write the date on a calendar and make sure you have access to a clock or watch.

Keeping Up Your Spirits

I am a believer that bringing positive energy and thoughts to tough situations can help achieve positive outcomes. So, while you are hospitalized, I'd like you to try and keep a positive outlook as best as you can.

I'm not trying to minimize your experience, nor am I suggesting that a false sense of cheerfulness will make every tough thing go away. I understand that you are sick. I understand that you may be in pain. I understand that you may have been given a life-changing diagnosis. All of those situations are real, and you have every right to every feeling of fear, anxiety, or anger that you may be experiencing.

I want to be clear that I'm not trying to tell anyone to look at things through rose-colored glasses and not assess the reality of their situation. Instead, I am advocating for you to hold on to whatever hope you have and think about what keeps you motivated to get better.

Maybe you want to get back to a hobby, work, or traveling. Be hopeful that you will one day get back to those things and use that hopeful drive to plan and participate in your recovery. Or maybe you find joy in another living being, and you want to return to them—your significant other, your children, or your pet. Please reach out to whomever puts a smile on your face, and let them know you need to hear their voice and laugh with them to keep your spirits up while you're on the mend. Or, if you're a spiritual person, please feel free to ask for the hospital's chaplain services, or invite your own spiritual leader to come to your bedside for fellowship together.

Ultimately, I'm not flippantly suggesting that you just "make the best out of a bad situation," but instead that you add hopefulness and a positive outlook as another tool in your treatment plan.

That being said, I understand that some people struggle with their mood before they even come into the hospital. Depression is a medical condition just like any other, and it should be treated as such.

Therefore, if you suffer from depression or have concerns that you are depressed, please tell your hospitalist or someone on your care team so that an appropriate medical plan can be made, which may include a consultation with the psychiatrist at the hospital. The same thing goes for if you ever feel as if you want to hurt yourself outside of or during your hospitalization.

Please immediately tell your care team if you are experiencing suicidal thoughts or ideas.

It might be easier for you to get in contact with a psychiatrist during your hospitalization than it will be outside the hospital. For that reason, take advantage of this resource. Not only can a mental health professional possibly start you on the appropriate medications, but they can also work with a social worker to help connect you with mental health resources after discharge.

Here are some ways to keep your spirits up:

- Keep a journal
- Keep in touch with loved ones
- Put up pictures of loved ones
- Do your daily grooming routine
- Ask your friends/family to visit
- Ask for a visit from the chaplain
- Get out of bed and walk around as much as possible
- Make plans for what you will do after you are discharged

Dr. Pich's Mental Health Corner

COMMUNICATING MENTAL HEALTH NEEDS TO THE PRIMARY TEAM

It is important to communicate any mental health needs you may have. This information includes any psychiatric or behavioral health conditions you are currently being treated for, your current medications, any substance use (alcohol, opiates, benzodiazepines) from which you may be at risk of withdrawal while in the hospital, and any past history of confusion or delirium when hospitalized.

1. Make sure that you are receiving all of your prescribed psychiatric medication while in the hospital, unless it has been discussed that they need to be held in the interim.
2. If you cannot recall all of your psychiatric medication, provide the contact information of your outpatient

treatment provider or pharmacy to the primary team so that they may obtain an accurate list.
3. If your psychiatric medication needs to be held for a procedure or other testing, ask when they will be started and have a plan for what to do if you start to experience worsening of any psychiatric symptoms.
4. Immediately inform the team if you have any unsafe thoughts about not wanting to live or wanting to hurt yourself or anyone else.
5. If you feel you or the primary team are not able to manage your mental health while in the hospital, request to have the psychiatric team provide a consultation.

Make Your Follow-Up Appointments Early

Setting up your follow-up appointments early is one of the best ways you can ensure your success post-hospitalization.

By day three or four, you're getting close to being able to leave the hospital. It's likely that you already know what you're going to need to do post-hospitalization, such as doing a post-hospitalization follow-up with your PCP or meeting with a specialist for a procedure.

The moment you learn whom you are to see after discharge, pull out your cell phone and call the offices of those providers. Make the appointments you need ASAP! Seriously, try it. It may be awhile before there is an appointment available with your PCP or specialists. I *always* tell my patients to call early, and it's been a huge help for them.

In some cases, the social worker or case manager can help set up complicated appointments or get you assistance with transportation needs, so feel free to ask for their help.

Seeing Specialists

The diagnosis and care plan that your hospitalist creates for you will include the additional support of a consulting physician (i.e., a specialist), if one is determined necessary. A surgical specialist is a physician who will evaluate you for any diagnosis that may necessitate surgical intervention and further management, a nonsurgical specialist is a physician who will give their highly specialized medical opinion on how to achieve a diagnosis and continue medical management. Also, some nonsurgical specialists do procedures that are not technically considered surgery, which can be both diagnostic in nature and also include interventions that are treatments.

On a similar note, if you already have a specific specialist you are seeing, there is a chance that you may not see that same specialist in the hospital. If you are admitted to a hospital where your specialist does not practice, you will be seen by the specialist available there. And if you happen to be admitted at the hospital where your specialist practices, you may either be seen by one of their partners or by your own physician, depending on their availability.

Last, I want to touch on the fact that you could be seeing a specialist for the first time if your hospitalist is concerned about a new diagnosis. Depending on your insurance and that specialist's availability, you may continue seeing that specialist after hospitalization or have to transfer care to someone within your insurance network.

Examples of Surgical and Nonsurgical Specialists

Surgical Specialists (not a complete list)	Nonsurgical Specialists (not a complete list)
• General Surgeons • Urologists • Surgical Oncologists • Cardiothoracic Surgeons • Otolaryngologists (a.k.a. Ear, Nose, and Throat Surgeons)	• Neurologists • Cardiologists • Infectious Disease Specialist • Oncologists

Family Meetings

Picture this: Your parent has been in the hospital for over five days. You feel like every question you've asked has led to even more confusing answers, and every new test and specialist leaves you more lost. Meanwhile, whenever you talk to your siblings, you gather that your older sister is just as confused and frustrated as you, while your younger brother seems to have a totally different set of wishes for your parent than you and your sister do.

What is your next step? How do you get all your questions answered? How do you get everyone on the same page?

When I sense that my patients and their loved ones are feeling as I've described above, I call for a family meeting. Family meetings are an incredible opportunity for you to stop, slow down, and get everyone invested in the patient together for a frank conversation so that you all are on the same page. At its core, a family meeting should give patients and their support system (loved ones, decision-makers, social and spiritual supports) an opportunity to directly communicate with the care team, collaborate on decisions, and set a clear path forward.

These meetings can be very challenging. Even so, since they are effective tools for communication and planning, they can pay off in dividends if everyone is properly prepared.

I've had some great family meetings, where we all hugged and wiped away tears of joy and relief at the end. These types of meetings happened because a sound medical and social plan that respected the patient's wishes had been agreed on. And...I've seen some go terribly wrong—where the disagreements between family members are intense, or the medical team gets berated because people feel out of control. Essentially, everyone involved ends up feeling worse than before the meeting. I've found that such scenarios happen when there are feelings of mistrust between various stakeholders, lack of clear communication, and unresolved questions around a patient's long-term goals.

I want to help you avoid the latter, which is why I've come up with this guide for effective family meetings. If you follow the four principals below, you should be able to come up with goals and a well-defined plan for the patient's care by the end of the session.

1. Define the Communication Goal: Why Are We Meeting?

Are you meeting because you feel lost in information? Or is it the opposite, that you don't feel as if you have enough information? Are you meeting because decisions need to be made, and you need input from other family members so that they can help you decide what to do next? Or are you meeting because you've gathered information from multiple sources, like specialists, and want your hospitalist to put it all together for you? Make sure you have a clearly defined answer to the "Why we are meeting?" question before going into the family meeting so that you actually accomplish your communication goals. Oftentimes, a family's reason for scheduling a meeting is "We're all confused, and we just want to hear it when we are all together." This communication goal is wonderful because a family meeting will allow everyone to hear the same information, ask questions, and hear the answers all at the same time.

2. Define the Key Stakeholders and Ensure They Are Present: Who Should Be There?

By *stakeholder*, I mean those who are actively part of the decision-making process, even if they are not the designated decision-maker. Remember, the number one person who needs to be there is the one who is legally designated as the decision-maker for the patient. (This is oftentimes the patient themselves.) As no decision is made in a vacuum, please be sure you have your support system present (i.e., anyone who is a source of comfort for you, can ask more in-depth questions, or can help you navigate the medical system). This is also a time when everybody who wants (and whom you want) to hear from the physician should make themselves available—luckily, in today's world, not everyone will actually have to come in person. Hospitals now have options for video calls and/or conference calls to be arranged.

If you have specific questions for members of the medical team other than the hospitalist, please ask that they attend, if possible. I've found that having various members of the medical team participate in the family meeting, alongside the primary hospitalist, can add more depth and understanding toward what exactly is happening with the patient. For example, a bedside nurse is a wonderful addition to a family meeting because they know the moment-to-moment needs and pains of the patient. Speech pathologists and physical therapists can also give very good information about someone's ability to eat safely and move around, as well as what their needs are going to be once they leave the hospital. It would be quite a boon if your specialist is able to attend a family meeting, but please don't be discouraged if specialists aren't in attendance. The hospitalist should be able to answer your questions, and you can schedule one-on-one calls with specialists at other times.

3. Ask for a Location That Suits Your Needs: When and Where Should the Meeting Occur?

Believe it or not, where you have your family meeting makes a huge difference. It often comes down to two options: a meeting room or by the patient's bedside. There are benefits to both (and sometimes you can do a hybrid by just asking to see the patient before or after your meeting), but generally speaking, a meeting room is comfortable and private, allows for conference and video calls, and can remove the decision-maker from a stressful environment.

On the other hand, having the meeting by the patient's bedside includes the patient, allows the family to see what kind of care is currently taking place, and gives a real picture of how the patient is feeling, coping, and progressing in their care. I have seen family members change their mind about some invasive treatments or code status after seeing the patient and realizing the patient is suffering more than they thought. The exact location is usually chosen the day of the meeting, depending on logistics and your preference between private rooms and bedside meetings.

I suggest that you schedule family meetings in the early afternoon. By the early afternoon, all necessary testing is usually done, labs and radiology results are back, and the hospitalist has likely had time to speak with specialists about the patient's care plan. When family members request a meeting early in the morning, I find that I have to call them back in the afternoon after the day has progressed just to rehash the earlier conversation but now without all the key stakeholders who were there before. Meetings that take place later in the day run the risk of being cut short due to shift changes or missing key providers who may have left the hospital for the day. Please try to avoid asking the nighttime providers for a family meeting as they are not likely to know the intimate details of the care plan and do not have access to the case managers, social workers, therapists, and other ancillary supports that providers during the day have. There may be times when an emergency meeting is needed at night, and these are usually initiated by the providers and nurses due to a change in medical condition.

Dr. Pieh's Mental Health Corner

WHAT TO DO WHEN YOU RECEIVE BAD NEWS

You may feel anxious or sad after hearing a new diagnosis or being given information about a prognosis. You may be surprised or shocked by what you learn. It is important to take time to process this information, and it may require an additional conversation with the treatment team.

1. Ask the team to explain what they have shared with you with as much detail as you need.
2. Ask to have a family member or other member of your support network present (if it would be helpful) to make sure you are fully informed of the information and what your or the patient's options are moving forward.
3. If you are struggling to cope with the news, consider asking to speak with the hospital chaplain, or reach out to your own pastor or priest if doing so might bring you comfort.

> 4. Receiving bad news may lead to feeling anxious or depressed, or it simply may make it difficult to sleep. Notify your primary team if you are experiencing any of these symptoms.

4. Have a Clear Plan for the Next Steps of Care: What Decisions Must Be Made by the End of the Family Meeting?

In addition to answering questions and resolving issues with communication, a good family meeting usually ends with some resolution to hard decisions that needed to be addressed. Some of the most common decisions that are made in a family meeting include the following:

- Reassessing code status
- Transitioning to an end-of-life care plan
- Deciding on placement after a hospitalization
- Deciding the need for conservatorship/guardianship
- Deciding whether to proceed with invasive procedures or high-risk medications

Hopefully, everyone leaves the family meeting having understood the goals not only for this hospitalization but also for longer-term plans. Keep in mind that if you feel no headway has been made after the family meeting—as though you've walked out of the room just as uninformed, confused, and frustrated as you were when you walked in—the next step would be to talk to a patient advocate. They will help you navigate whatever roadblocks you feel you're facing.

I would also like to note that you should absolutely ask for a translator if English is not the language you or others in the meeting are most comfortable speaking. Hospitals must provide a translator who is not a loved one, and this service can take place in person, over the phone, or virtually.

With all that I've just said, I hope you see the value of family meetings. They really are a great way to get all parties tied to the patient on the same page and to foster communication and problem-solving.

I believe that some of my best work as a physician has happened in family meetings, because these sessions have really helped me understand a patient's goals, values, and expectations, along with their family's hopes and capabilities.

Most times, family meetings allow the parties to come to decisions that then drive the rest of the hospitalization. Being able to assist patients and their families in creating a care plan that will give them comfort, honor their values, and accomplish their goals is why I love my job—and family meetings help me do just that.

> **REAL TALK:**
>
> **FAMILY MEETINGS ARE HARD**
>
> Family meetings are stressful, so please try to be nice.
>
> Everybody participating in the family meeting is bringing their own set of ideas, values, and expectations. Strained interpersonal dynamics that existed before are likely to feel amplified in a stressful meeting. So, I am asking that you do your best to bring an open mind and heart to a family meeting. Try to take a

step back, hear what others are saying, and see what value you can find in it.

Truthfully, it's rare that one party is 100% correct and that the other is 100% wrong. Most times, everyone is trying to bring their best intentions and hopes to the table. If things start to get a bit testy, I ask that you take a deep breath and try to be the calming voice in the room that brings everyone back to focus on what really matters: the patient.

Part Six: Day Five

Leaving the Hospital

It's been a long journey, and you or your loved one is finally nearing the end of their hospitalization. But now what?

Though going directly home after the hospital is preferred, it may not be the safest place to go next. Therefore, in this chapter, we are going to cover the many places one could go after being discharged and any planning required to make that happen:

- Post–Acute Care Facilities
    - Skilled Nursing Facilities
    - Short-Term Rehabilitation Centers
    - Long-Term Acute Care Facilities
    - Long-Term Care Centers
- Transfer to Another Acute Hospital
- Hospice: End-of-Life Care After Discharge
    - Home Hospice
    - Hospice House/Center
    - Hospice in the Hospital
- Getting Ready to Leave
- "Home" May Look Different
- The Logistics of Leaving
- Welcome Home

We will also discuss the logistics of leaving and the fact that being at home may look and feel different from before.

Leaving the hospital can come with a set of new, unique challenges that you've likely never even thought about, and sometimes, hard decisions have to be made. My hope is that this chapter will prepare you for all of it.

I'm sure you're excited to leave the hospital, so let's get to it!

Post-Acute Care Facilities

After discharge from the hospital, some people will require more prolonged, intensive care or therapies than they can get at home, so they will have to go to a place that can do those things for them. I like to think of these facilities as a pit stop in between a hospital and the home.

These facilities are designed for patients who don't require the level of intensive care that is given in the hospital, but they still aren't well enough to be home yet or cannot safely get a needed treatment at home.

The facilities will be referred to as the following:

- **Skilled nursing facilities (SNF)**: Don't think of a skilled nursing facility as a nursing home, because the treatment received at an SNF is meant to end at some point. In order to go to a skilled nursing facility, you have to have what we refer to as a skilled nursing need—essentially an issue that can only be handled by a nurse with the proper training and/or equipment (e.g., frequent or complex wound care).[78]
- **Short-term rehabilitation facilities**: Your stay in a short-term rehabilitation facility is meant to be temporary and intense, focusing on getting you strong enough to go home—which is why I do not consider such a facility to be a nursing home either. To be at a short-term rehab,

---

[78] "Medicare Coverage for Inpatient Rehabilitation," AARP Medicare Plans, accessed March 22, 2022, https://www.aarpmedicareplans.com/medicare-articles/medicare-coverage-for-inpatient-rehabilitation.html.

you have to be well enough to participate in PT for your recovery—making it a perfect stop for those who aren't quite ready to go home because they are still too weak to be alone in their home or to navigate the infrastructure of home (e.g., too weak to climb stairs safely). In these cases, short-term rehabilitation serves as a mediating stop to get a patient stronger. It also allows patients to learn how to use new equipment that they need to make their safe and triumphant return home.

- **Long-term care (LTC)**: This is a nursing home, where patients receive custodial care (i.e., help with everyday activities such as eating and dressing). Someone would head to a long-term care facility if they could not do those things for themselves and could not be cared for in the home. Typically, the process of getting someone's personal effects and legal/financial affairs in line so that they can afford an LTC facility tends to take longer than the four to five days of a typical hospitalization. Thus, your case manager at the hospital may suggest that the necessary paperwork for transitioning to a long-term care facility be started in the hospital and completed while the patient is at either a short-term rehab or a skilled nursing facility. All of these post–acute care facilities will have case managers who can help continue the process of getting someone into a long-term care facility for custodial care.[79]
- **Long-term acute care hospital**: This is like a nursing home for people who have high medical needs—kind of

---

79 "What Is the Difference Between a Skilled Nursing Facility and a Nursing Home?," AARP Medicare Plans from Universal Healthcare, accessed February 20, 2022, https://www.aarpmedicareplans.com/medicare-articles/whats-the-difference-between-a-skilled-nursing-facility-and-a-nursing-home.html.

like a smaller acute hospital where someone can be long term (e.g., someone with a tracheostomy who is bedbound may live in an LTAC).[80]

With the exception of the long-term acute care hospital, the above post–acute care facilities are a lower level of medical intensity compared to hospital care. Each place is designed to fit a niche care need, making such choices perfect for people who can't go home after the hospital temporarily or permanently. I know it's a bit tempting to call them all nursing homes, so I hope you now have an understanding of their differences and know which one may be relevant to your needs.

The place that you or your loved one goes to will be facilitated by your case manager, who will help you make the decision that best suits your needs. So, make sure you're as honest as possible with the case manager about your or the patient's needs, whether home is a safe environment for you/them, and if you/they will have the assistance required there to be safe.

Of course, it's never easy to go to one of these facilities or to put your loved one in one, especially when it comes to long-term care. Many people find themselves trying to avoid it, because the thought of going home is much more comforting. In fact, research has found that people can do better at home with appropriate supports, so ask what you will need to safely be in the home, and see how feasible it all is.[81]

---

80 "Long Term Acute Care Hospital (LTACH)," Emory Healthcare, accessed March 22, 2022, https://www.emoryhealthcare.org/ui/pdfs/continuing-care-forms/post-acute-level-of-care-ltach-level-of-care-faq.pdf?msclkid=318cfa59a66c11eca62ba8c3d5289902.

81 "Program of All-Inclusive Care for the Elderly (PACE)," Centers for Medicare & Medicaid Services, December 1, 2021, https://www.cms.gov/Medicare-Medicaid-Coordination/Medicare-and-Medicaid-Coordination/Medicare-Medicaid-Coordination-Office/PACE/PACE.

Say you live alone in a two-story home but have trouble walking up stairs during your inpatient PT evaluation. Going home in this case—without having additional care to get you up and down the stairs—could be a major risk to your safety. Similarly, if your loved one requires 24-hour supervision and can't be left at home alone due to dementia, they may need to go to one of these facilities to ensure their safety.

I know it's never easy to make these decisions, but it really does come down to safety.

It's also important to consider the financial implications of going to a post–acute care facility because, depending on the nursing need and the length of time needed, things can be expensive. Please lean on your case manager to help you navigate your health insurance benefits for post-acute care and other avenues to help with any associated costs.

> **PRO TIP FOR POST-ACUTE CARE FACILITIES:** Send your care partner to tour a facility.

I always suggest that somebody visit the post–acute care facility options to which the patient might be going. Everything looks different in a brochure or on a website, and these facilities are no different. Having someone tour the facility will give a better idea of what the physical space is like, how friendly the staff is, and what the general vibe of the place is. If you'll be the patient there, you'll want a place where you can be comfortable and where your friends and family have easy access. All hospitalists know of cases where patients return to the hospital shortly after leaving because they refuse to get off the stretcher once they arrive at the facility for one reason or another. Try to avoid surprises by having someone you trust do a tour of the facility while you are hospitalized.

Transfer to Another Acute Hospital

If you can remember back to "Pre-Day One" in this book, we talked about transfers that arose from preference and/or your medical needs (e.g., being transferred to the hospital where you are receiving cancer care). Now we are going to discuss what happens when you need to be transferred to a different hospital after being hospitalized for a few days already.

The chances of you being transferred to another acute care hospital during your current hospitalization like being transferred to another hospital from the emergency department depends on the medical necessity of said transfer, and bed availability at the accepting hospital.

At some point in your hospitalization, it may become clear to your care team that it is necessary for you to be transferred to another hospital where you can receive care by specialist or get an intervention that your current hospital doesn't have. This is what we refer to as a patient needing "higher level or care."

Remember, not every hospital does every type of intervention or has every specialist,

> **Common Reasons for Interhospital Transfers**
> - Specialized Interventions (e.g., Endovascular Neurosurgery)
> - Specialized Teams for Complex Illnesses (e.g., Bone Marrow Transplants)
> - Specialized Surgeries (e.g., Transplant Services)

because it is not possible to retain those resources across every hospital in the country. So, if your medical needs are better served by a different hospital an interhospital transfer will be facilitated.

How quickly you can be transferred depends on the number of open beds at the accepting hospital. Sometimes it may take several days for the appropriate bed to open up for a transfer to take place.

Psychiatric Hospitalizations

The last type of interhospital transfer I want to touch on is for psychiatric care. Psychiatric hospitals are specially designed to stabilize patients in acute psychiatric crisis and can deliver more aggressive pharmacologic management of mental illness than is available at a medical hospital. These hospitals have the capability of dealing with more-severe psychiatric illnesses and psychiatric emergencies, and they deliver specialized treatments under the care of psychiatrists. It is not uncommon for a patient who is coming in for a medical hospitalization to need both medical and psychiatric care, so if a patient's medical needs have been met, but the patient still needs active psychiatric management, they will be transferred to a psychiatric hospital directly.

Unfortunately, inpatient psychiatric hospitals are not very numerous, so patients may wait several days to be transferred and/or may have to be sent to a psychiatric hospital far away.

When these transfers do happen, they are coordinated under the direction of the psychiatric team and may include some assistance from the social worker or case manager.

Before we conclude speaking about transfers, I want to emphasize that a mid-hospitalization transfer doesn't mean the hospital where you were was not a good hospital or that it was not the right hospital for you to have started your care in. In fact, I see it as quite the opposite: you were at a hospital where all the necessary diagnoses and treatments were done to stabilize your problem, and you will continue your treatment at a different hospital that can deliver the more specialized care that you were determined to need.

Managing Pain and Other Symptoms at the End of Life: Palliative Care versus Hospice Care

When there are no further curative options, the next step in management is to focus on symptom control, allowing a patient to pass with comfort and dignity. At this point in their care, the patient is usually introduced to a different group of providers—who are experts in palliative and hospice care—to help the team focus on the goal of comfort. Palliative care can encompass hospice, but it is not solely focused on hospice care. Let's discuss the difference between the two in a bit more depth.

Palliative care physicians are specially trained to help manage all symptoms of pain and discomfort at any point in a patient's illness, which can include end of life.

Patients can be introduced to palliative care at any time in their illnesses, not just when someone is dying.[82] Working with palliative care doesn't mean that you will immediately be transitioning to hospice. It just means that you need someone to focus on your symptoms of pain or discomfort. Palliative care teams can also help navigate complicated medical decisions to help you set reasonable goals of care and to respect your wishes for care at all

---

82 Katherine Kim, "When Is Palliative Care Appropriate?," WebMD, November 30, 2021, https://www.webmd.com/palliative-care/when-is-palliative-care-appropriate.

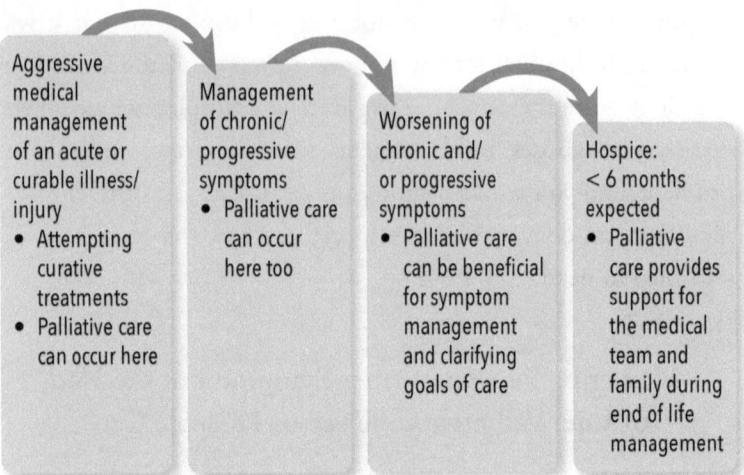

Palliative care: supporting patients at any stage of treatment

times. If at any time a patient or physician feels that long-term symptom management will need to be addressed, a palliative care provider can be of assistance.

Hospice care occurs when it is determined that a person is terminally ill and will likely die sometime in the near future.[83] Hospice is a service built to support someone who is actively passing away.

For reference, this simple question determines whether someone is an appropriate candidate for hospice or not: Would I reasonably expect that this person will be alive within the next six months? If the answer is no, hospice is appropriate.

---

83   "What Is Hospice Care?," American Cancer Society, accessed February 20, 2022, https://www.cancer.org/treatment/end-of-life-care/hospice-care/what-is-hospice-care.html.

End-of-Life Care After Discharge: Hospice

Caring for someone during the end of their life is as important and as active a process as any other type of care we give patients. When it is decided that the goals of care for a patient are no longer to attempt curative medical interventions but rather to focus on relieving pain and suffering to support a person who is dying, hospice becomes the most appropriate type of care your medical team can deliver.

The following information is going to be very important for you if you or a loved one is considering hospice. We will go over the different locations that hospice can occur, which are as follows:

- At Home
- At a Facility
    - Hospice Center (a.k.a. Hospice House or Respite House)
    - Skilled Nursing Facility
    - Long-Term Care Facility
- In the Hospital

Hospice at Home

If given the choice, most people would prefer to die at home surrounded by their loved ones. Hospice at home gives families the chance to honor a patient's wishes and also allows them to be active participants in the last days of their loved ones.

Therefore, home hospice can be a really wonderful and comforting experience for all involved, but there is also one thing about hospice care at home that I want you to be mindful of: Hospice care at home doesn't guarantee around-the-clock care by medical professionals. If family/friends are not able to adequately care for their dying loved one at home, home hospice can be cumbersome or may not be possible.

Going home with hospice usually means that the patient's family members will have to provide care about 22 to 23 hours a day, which means that those at home with the patient will be doing all of the toileting, feeding, and turning, as well as giving pain medications. Many hospice services will send a nurse into the home, but it's typically only for a short amount of time each day. Having a nurse in the home 24 hours a day tends to be a private service that requires direct out-of-pocket payments rather than being covered by health insurance.

When deciding on home hospice, it is vital that you speak openly and honestly with your case manager about the following considerations:

- The needs of the person who is dying at home
- Services and the amount of time in the home that the hospice team will provide
- What the family will be expected to do
- Supplemental things that insurance covers
- Additional services available in the community or that may require direct payments

Speaking openly will be critical because, just like everything else I've talked about in this book, the most important thing about home hospice is safety. It can be dangerous for a person on home hospice to be taken care of by someone ill-equipped to do so. Unwanted outcomes like falling, medication errors, or choking on food can happen. These events can unfortunately cause unwanted pain and suffering and may even hasten someone's death beyond the disease process for which they are on hospice.

So, if you or your support team have concerns that accommodating hospice care at home might be difficult, but you still want to do it, the one thing I really want you to do is to have an open and honest dialogue with your care team (particularly the case manager) about why exactly you/they feel unsure about home hospice. Furthermore, I want you to clearly state what the caregiver's capabilities are and their comfort level with delivering medical care.

I urge you to seriously consider all of those concerns, because the last thing I want to happen is to have the patient return to the hospital because of uncontrolled pain, unaddressed symptoms, or an unforeseen safety issue. Anytime I have seen any of those things happen, all parties involved in the case end up frustrated, sad, and feeling like a failure. Home hospice can be a beautiful experience—but only if you are set up and supported to do it. So, please, ask for all the help you think you will need.

REAL TALK:

CAREGIVER FATIGUE IS REAL
Do your best to take care of all parties participating in home hospice. Allow caregivers to take breaks, find support during the night so that people can sleep, and bring over food so that everyone can eat.

> If you need it, reach out to your therapist, clergy, support group, or best friends to have a safe place for processing grief. Try to create space and time for any children (teenagers included) who may be in the home to tell you what they need to feel comfortable with home hospice. Children will likely need more specific support to process their grief, so ask your pediatrician for guidance on what programs are available in your area.

Now, if it has been decided that hospice will be happening at home, you will need to make arrangements to accommodate everything and everyone needed to support the patient. There will often be a point in the process of preparing for home hospice when people tell me they feel "too rushed" to leave the hospital and go home. I never want you to feel as if you have to hurry out of the hospital, but if you are feeling rushed, it's usually because of one of two things:

1. **The patient is likely going to pass away soon, and it may not be possible to coordinate home hospice in time.** It's never ideal to have someone die very shortly after arriving home, so if you feel like this may happen, it is time to have a conversation with your hospitalist about transitioning to comfort care within the hospital.
2. **You are not logistically and/or emotionally ready to bring a dying person into the home.** I always tell family members who are feeling this way to pick a day that they think they will be ready to go home with hospice and then expect to leave the day after that. You'll have a lot

of work to do, and no matter how well you prepare, you may find that something is going to slow you down. To help get you started, here are some basic areas that need to be covered:

- Schedule equipment and medication delivery time
- If bedrooms are upstairs, consider reconfiguring the home to accommodate first-floor living
- Move furniture to accommodate a hospital bed and any other necessary equipment
- Print a list of important phone numbers, and tape it up in a central place
- Create a shift schedule for caregivers
- Decide on how you will accommodate visitors…*if* you decide to accommodate visitors (don't feel pressured to do so)

Hopefully, the above guide helps you think about what else you need to do to accommodate hospice at home.

Hospice at a Facility

There are specific facilities dedicated to the care of people at the end of their lives. I'll refer to such places as hospice houses, but they may also be known as respite houses (sometimes they'll also temporarily care for a patient, giving home caregivers much-needed breaks).[84]

These facilities tend to be really beautiful, quiet, peaceful places that are staffed by people for whom hospice care is their

---

84 "What Is Respite Care?," National Institute on Aging, May 1, 2017, https://www.nia.nih.gov/health/what-respite-care.

life calling. Oftentimes, people will say that they prefer their loved one to go to a facility like this, particularly if they feel that they can't care for them at home.

This decision is again where a frank conversation with your case manager is necessary to find out what is covered by your insurer. I hope you find the facilities and community supports that will allow your loved one to be in the hospice house of your choosing.

Another type of facility, besides hospice houses, where people pass away are some of the ones we talked about earlier, like long-term care facilities and skilled nursing facilities. A skilled nursing facility may be right for the patient if they need more-intensive nursing attention to address specific symptoms and continue aggressive pain management.

On the other hand, those who have lived in long-term care facilities for many years become quite comfortable there, so passing away there may be akin to dying at home. If that's the case for the patient, talk to the case manager at both the hospital and at the facility to see if they could support hospice in that long-term care facility.

Hospice in the Hospital: Transitioning to Comfort Measure/Comfort Care

If someone is asked where they'd like to die, very few people actually say that they would like to die in the hospital. Unfortunately, the reality is that a lot of people in the U.S. pass away there.

Personally, I think we're culturally set up to understand that when someone experiences a catastrophic event, like getting hit by a car, they might die in the hospital. It's unexpected, yet somehow easy to wrap the mind around. But many times, it's harder for us to accept that someone who has medical complications and/or declining health can die in the hospital.

After all, most of us think of hospitals as places where people get better, not worse and then die. In these cases, the patient's illness either progressed quickly due to acute worsening of their chronic/progressive illness or their illness progressed to the point that further treatment would no longer yield improvement and would be futile. You may think you should be prepared for someone with a chronic or progressive illness to die, but it is impossible to be totally prepared to lose someone you love.

Thankfully, hospitals have systems and protocols set up to support patients and their loved ones through the process of someone dying in the hospital. Once it is decided that the goals of care will transition to supporting comfort and relieving symptoms while the patient dies, you may find the term *comfort measures* being said. This term means that all treatments will be geared toward comfort, and anything that can cause discomfort (e.g., blood draws) or doesn't add to the goal of comfort (e.g., taking daily medications that aren't for pain/discomfort) will be stopped. Oxygen and IV fluids may be removed as well, as these are no longer appropriate treatments and may cause discomfort in some cases. Last, monitors may be removed or turned off as it brings nobody any comfort to watch the moment-to-moment vital signs of a dying person.

Each patient is different, so please sit down and discuss the plan for comfort measures with your hospitalist. That way, you can clearly understand what treatments will and will not be given. Some hospitals may have designated rooms for those who are on comfort measures, but oftentimes, you will find that care will be continued in the same room where the patient already is.

The top priority for the care team at this point then becomes comfort. Because those who are dying oftentimes cannot speak, there are going to be signs and symptoms of discomfort the care team will look for:

- Rigid Posture
- Moaning/Groaning
- Sweating
- Rapid or Uncomfortable-Looking Breathing Patterns
- Facial Grimacing
- Scared Facial Expressions
- Clenched Hands
- Vomiting or Retching

The above are indicators that the patient's symptoms of pain and other forms of discomfort have not been controlled adequately. If that's the case, you may notice your care team prescribe medications to help the patient become more comfortable, free from pain or anxiety. Spend some time discussing exactly what medications will be used to achieve the patient's comfort so that everyone is up to date and agrees with the care plan. Nursing care for wounds, drains, urinary catheters, etc. should also continue as appropriate to help the patient be more comfortable.

Pro Tips for Comfort Care in the Hospital

- Change your expectations to accept relieving pain and suffering, not prolonging life.
- Do not look at the monitors or ask for vital signs to be checked. These do not give any indication of when a person will die and can be emotionally triggering.
- Ask for a palliative care consult if you feel that the patient's

pain management plan isn't sufficient.
- If you'd like any religious support, you may ask for it. The chaplain is usually made aware of these patients as well.
- Ask if there is any capability to extend visiting hours or increase the number of visitors allowed in the room.
- Be prepared that your regular hospitalist may not be present when your loved one dies. The death examination and certificate may be completed by another physician if your loved one dies when your hospitalist is not there.
- You may step out of the room for the death examination. Do not feel that you have to stay and watch.

Getting Ready to Leave

By day five, you're probably itching to leave the hospital, so let's get you prepped to go. There are a few things you should be aware of that will help you navigate this process more easily:

1. Logistics: who, when, how?
2. Getting your new medications
3. At-home services and new equipment
4. Paperwork

It's time to move on to logistics—the who, the when, and the how of leaving the hospital.

1. Logistics

a. Who is picking you up? Most patients need a ride home. Very few people drive themselves to the hospital or are well enough to drive themselves home. My suggestion is that your care partner be the person picking you up from the hospital. This way you both can go over all the discharge instructions and the new medication list with your nurse. This will be your last chance to get questions answered about your post-discharge care plan, which is why I suggest your care partner be there if possible.

b. When are you being discharged? Before being discharged, a final meeting with your case manager should take place to go over the details of your discharge. Again, this is your opportunity to ask any final questions about your post-hospitalization plan.

c. How are you leaving the hospital? If you need specialized medical transportation, like an ambulance or chair car, to get home, all of those arrangements will be made for you, so your care partner will need to be involved to ensure that someone will be at home to receive you when you arrive.

If you are going to a post–acute care facility, the hospital will arrange for your transportation there.

2. Getting Your New Medications

The medication reconciliation process that was done upon your arrival will be repeated again at the time of discharge, and your nurse will review the updated medication list with you. Some hospitals may have someone from the pharmacy team stop by to review your updated medication list with you. This is the time to ask all your questions and make sure you understand how your medication list changed from what you were taking prior to admission. Most prescriptions, including those for controlled substances, can be sent to your pharmacy via electronic prescriptions, which is a wonderful thing for three reasons: (1) You won't lose that prescription; (2) your pharmacy can price the medicine before you get there and advise you of the cost, which is a bonus because if you have any issues with affording your medication, you can use the hospital's case manager to find another way to access it; and (3) your prescription can be ready and waiting for you when you get to the pharmacy.

Another recommendation I have for medications is to not use a mail-in pharmacy because you'll likely need your new medication the same day you leave the hospital. If you use a mail-in pharmacy, it will take several days for the prescription to reach you in the mail. So, if you regularly use a mail-in pharmacy, you should ask your physician in the hospital for a 30-day prescription sent to a local pharmacy, and then ask your primary care doctor to transition said prescription over to your mail-in pharmacy.

I especially want to address the topic of a prescription for oxygen because it can be tricky. Oxygen can be a temporary treatment for some, while it may be more permanent for others. Remember to treat oxygen as you do all prescriptions: use it as directed on the prescription. If you are instructed to wear oxygen at all times, wear it at all times, not just when you feel short of breath. Oxygen is a lifesaving medication, so please use it as directed. Remember two important safety points about having oxygen in the home: (1) don't smoke around oxygen, and (2) take care not to trip on the tubing.

3. At-Home Services and New Equipment

Now, the bulk of most patients' recoveries will take place at home, and some people may really benefit from at-home medical care and new equipment to ensure that they can be safe at home and continue to get well.

If you are able to go home, there might be a chance that you will leave with new services and/or equipment. I do want you to expect to go home with some new medication—that's the most likely thing to happen—but there's still a probability you could go home needing a few larger items.

I want you to treat any new equipment you are given as a prescription that is just as important for your care and safety as any pill. Please make sure you know how you're going to get your hands on the new equipment post-hospitalization, if it is not already given to you in the hospital. Things like a shower chair or bedside commode can be bought without a prescription, but if you need insurance to pay for it, you may need to get it at specified locations.

I cannot drive home enough how important it is that you *use* any newly prescribed assistive devices, particularly walkers and canes. There is nary a week that I don't admit to the hospital a patient who fell because they didn't use their walker or cane. I've met many elderly patients who prefer to do what I call "furniture hopping," moving from couch to table and so forth with their hands as their only support. This is not a safe way to get around the house and will eventually lead to an injury. Who knows, you may just need to bedazzle your walker and give it some flair to be more confident with using it.

Shower chairs are another piece of equipment people are hesitant to use, but I cannot stress enough how imperative they are for safety. Falls in the bathroom can be extremely dangerous or even catastrophic.[85] Shower chairs not only help a person avoid falls, but they also allow you to maintain hygiene—which will ultimately get you back on track with your regular activities.

Let's move onto the *services* part of *at-home services and equipment*. This area is pretty much what it sounds like: medical services you can receive at home.

Surprisingly, a lot of healthcare can be delivered in the home—some hospitalizations can even be done at home at lower costs, and many people have very good outcomes. The takeaway here is you can actually get a lot of treatment done in your home, so feel free to ask if these are options for you at any point in your hospitalization.[86]

---

85 "Nonfatal Bathroom Injuries Among Persons Aged >15 Years—United States, 2008," *Morbidity and Mortality Weekly Report* 60, no. 11 (June 10, 2011): 729–733, https://www.cdc.gov/mmwr/preview/mmwrhtml/mm6022a1.htm.
86 "Creating Value by Bringing Hospital Care Home," American Hospital Association, December 2020, https://www.aha.org/system/files/media/file/2020/12/issue-brief-creating-value-by-bringing-hospital-care-home_0.pdf.

Such services might be provided by a visiting nurse, PT/OT practitioners, etc. If you believe you are in need of some at-home care, please ask your case manager if you qualify. The worst thing they can say is no!

Below are examples of medical care that can be given at home (not a complete list):

- IV Medications (e.g., Antibiotics)
- Infusion Pumps (e.g., Pain Meds)[87]
- Wound Care (e.g., Vacuums, Drains)[88]
- Urinary Catheters[89]
- Peritoneal Dialysis or Hemodialysis[90]

We now have the ability to do surprisingly intensive care at home, which is a huge perk of healthcare today. This capability may even be the future of medicine, so take advantage of whatever at-home care you can receive!

4. Paper Work

If you need something like a return-to-work/school note, please let your hospitalist know prior to your leaving the hospital because, once you are discharged, it may be difficult for you to get in touch with the hospitalist who treated you. Some paperwork,

---

[87] "Home Infusion Therapy Services," Center for Medicare & Medicaid Services, accessed February 20, 2020, https://www.cms.gov/Medicare/Medicare-Fee-for-Service-Payment/Home-Infusion-Therapy/Overview.

[88] "Wound Vac in Home Health Care," Professional Home Care Services Inc., August 26, 2021, https://www.phcsonline.com/blog1/wound-vac-home-health-care/.

[89] "Living with a Urinary Catheter," NHS, updated February 26, 2020, https://www.nhs.uk/conditions/urinary-catheters/living-with/.

[90] "Home Hemodialysis," National Kidney Foundation, accessed February 20, 2022, https://www.kidney.org/atoz/content/homehemo.

like disability claims, may be more appropriately completed by your PCP or a specialist after discharge when the total extent of your illness and limitations are better understood.

Paperwork frequently requested at discharge includes return-to-work notes, light-duty notes, or last-dose letters for those enrolled in opiate-replacement therapy.

Dr. Pieh's Mental Health Corner

PREPARING TO GO HOME

The anticipation of returning home can create significant anxiety and worry, which is why it is important to know what the plan is for returning home.

- Ask to speak with the treatment team and unit case manager/social worker if there are specific concerns. Include family or support network members in this conversation.
- Clarify if you will need to schedule outpatient follow-ups for any appointments or if they will be scheduled for you.
- Clarify any changes in your medication regimen—including what was stopped and why, what was started and why, or if anything will need to be restarted once you are home.
- Ensure that prescriptions were sent to your pharmacy and that you will be able to pick them up in a timely manner. If there are any concerns about not being able to pick up your prescriptions, notify the team.

"Home" May Look Different

If you are able to leave the hospital and go home with the intention of taking care of yourself, you're in a great spot.

Even though you're able to be at home with your loved ones and can take care of yourself, your home might still look different. Perhaps you have new medications, new equipment, or even in-home services, like PT.

Not to mention that, as I've said time and time again, you will not be feeling as if you are back to 100%. Some people have a hard time accepting that they can be discharged without feeling totally back to normal, but the truth is that sometimes the safest place to continue your care and rehabilitation is not the hospital, and there is always the possibility that a protracted hospitalization can actually do more harm than good.

As a general way to estimate how long it'll be before you feel normal again, may I suggest that "for every one day you're in the hospital, it may take you one week to feel better." When I was a resident, one of my attending physicians used to say this to patients, and I've found that this equation is actually pretty accurate. For example, if you've been in the hospital for four days, it's going to take you about a month to really get back to your full form.

But even more important than that is putting in the work required for your recovery. To reiterate the previous parts of this chapter, here are the areas where some adjustments may need to be made in your lifestyle:

- New equipment (e.g., walker, cane, bedside commode, wound care supplies)

- New medications (your discharge medication list compared with what you were taking prior to being hospitalized)
- New diet (e.g., low salt, low sugar, soft textures)
- Support in the home (e.g., part-time or full-time help by family, friends, or professionals)
- New doctors (e.g., continued care with the new specialists)

Please take care of yourself and follow the directions on your discharge paperwork: Go to PT, take the medications prescribed to you, use the equipment given to you, and follow your prescribed diet. *Do the work.*

It may not be easy, but your recovery will only be prolonged if you don't—which puts you at risk for another hospitalization. I see a huge difference in patients who are active participants in their care and rehabilitation versus those who go home and try to immediately return to their previous lifestyle or those who do not participate in their convalescing and get worse.

I know it's hard, but you are worth the effort. Yes, it may take you several attempts to make these adjustments and really stick to them, so give yourself some time and space to discover what works for you.

The Logistics of Leaving

They tend not to show this part in movies, but leaving the hospital is a process. You're not just going to be able to get up and walk out the door. First, there are going to be three people with whom you have to meet before you can leave:

1. **Your hospitalist**: On the last day of your hospitalization, your hospitalist will make sure you've improved enough, are medically stable, and have a safe discharge plan in place so that you are safe to leave. When you see your hospitalist on the day of discharge, I want you to take out your list of questions and ask every single question you have left. It's really now or never—after discharge, your hospitalist may no longer be able to provide some types of care, and you may have to wait to see your PCP to have issues addressed. Remember when I said it may be difficult for your hospitalist to complete paperwork if you're not in the hospital anymore? This meeting is also when you should make sure you have all your employment, school, last-dose, insurance, etc. papers sorted out and signed if you haven't already.
2. **Your nurse**: Your nurse will be the person who can remove your IV line, heart monitor, urinary catheter, and anything else necessary so that you are no longer physically tethered to the hospital. The nurse will also be the person who reviews your list of discharge medications. I understand written instructions may not always be easy to understand, so please ask lots of questions and take

lots of notes. Some hospitals may have someone from the pharmacy review the discharge medication list with you instead; if so, know that this person is a great resource, so ask lots of questions and take notes. Finally, your nurse will also go over how to carry out necessary care in the home. For example, if you are new to using insulin, your nurse will show you how to draw up and administer the insulin to yourself.

3. **Your case manager**: This meeting will be very essential because the case manager is going to cover the logistics of your discharge and post-hospitalization care. They will schedule things such as equipment deliveries, specialized medication orders, at-home care, transitions to a facility for further care, and so on. Since they're also coordinating with your insurance, the case manager will be handling the logistics of your medication authorizations and working through any potential hurdles that arise, like finding an alternative way for you to get medications your insurance doesn't cover. As always, ask every question you have and take note of everything your case manager says. Your understanding is imperative to the success of your recovery. I also want to note this: I understand you may be really excited to leave the hospital, but this is where I'm going to ask you to have a little patience. Your case manager is probably working diligently to find solutions for you, and you cannot leave the hospital without a complete discharge plan.

Once all of these meetings are completed, you're ready to get out of the hospital. That's great news, but *how*? How are you leaving?

I know this point may seem like a minor question, but it's actually a really important one because there are many routes you could take. Think about some of the options you'll have:

1. **Driving yourself**: This is only an option for those who (a) are able to operate a car, and (b) drove themselves to the hospital, so their car is already available.
2. **Getting a ride from a friend or family member**: This is typically safe for those who are able to get in and out of a car, either by themselves or with the assistance of the driver. As previously mentioned, it is ideal if the person who picks you up is a care partner who can join in and listen to the discharge instructions and review the discharge paperwork.
3. **Getting a taxi**: Like above, this option is only for people who can get in and out of a car without much assistance. You will also need some way of getting into your home, so be sure that you have your keys or that someone is home to let you in. The taxi ride might be covered by the hospital, so make sure you talk to your case manager if you need one.
4. **Getting an ambulance**: Ambulance rides home or to a facility are for people who have complex medical needs, cannot get in or out of a car, and need assistance to physically get into the home or facility. If an ambulance ride is necessary for discharge, the case manager will coordinate all the logistics.

No matter what your preference is, make sure you talk to your case manager about how you're leaving. They will find the best method of transportation for you or your loved one to the next stop, whether that be home or a facility.

Dr. Pich's Mental Health Corner

OUTPATIENT OR COMMUNITY RESOURCES

Discuss with the primary team, particularly with the social worker/case manager, if you have any psychosocial needs that may make it difficult for you to return home.

- Contact your health insurance company to inquire about any services covered. There are often resources available, particularly related to the transition back home, including assistance with rides to appointments, home-based support, or other needs. The social worker or case manager may also be able to assist with finding out what resources are covered by your insurance.
- For outpatient psychiatric or mental health resources, determine the time to wait for an appointment (if any).
- Ensure you have enough medication to last until your follow-up appointment.

Welcome Home

You found your way home or to your new post–acute care facility—congratulations and best wishes with your recovery!

You'll probably find that you have new instructions on how to care for yourself now that you're out of the hospital. Those instructions could be related to medication, diet, movement—really everything we've talked about in this book so far. Follow the instructions until you see your primary care physician, who may make some adjustments depending on how you're progressing.

The first thing I want you to do when you get home is to *repeat the medication reconciliation process.* If you're at a facility, medications will be managed for you, so you won't have to worry about this task until you are discharged home, at which point you should do it again.

At-home medication reconciliation is critical to your safety and also happens to be where a lot of people can get confused. Let's make sure you're not one of those cases.

Now, upon leaving the hospital, you should receive something like the following form. I want you to go to wherever you keep your medications and take out every medicine you have, old and new, and even the ones you've been saving for some unknown reason.

Medication Reconciliation: Discharge List

Name	Taking at Home	Continue in Hospital	New During Hospitalization	Continue at Home
Ibuprofen	Yes	No		No
Metoprolol	Yes	No		Yes
Loratadine	Yes	No		Yes
Ceftriaxone	No	___	Yes	No
Acetaminophen	No	___	Yes	Yes

When you're done taking out your medications, make three piles:

1. **Medicines you need to stop taking**: These are medications that are either not on your medication list from the hospital or are labeled as *Stop Taking* on that list. Put these in a bag and take them to your local pharmacy to be disposed of if your primary care physician agrees that you will never again take those medicines. I suggest that people dispose of old medications because there's always a chance you may accidentally take them if they remain in the home. While you're at it, make sure you dispose of any expired prescriptions. No more antibiotics from 1993, please!

2. **Medicines you need to be taking**: These are medications that the list instructs you to take. Some will be new. Some will be the ones you were already taking prior to your hospitalization. Put these in a safe, accessible place so you can take them as prescribed.

3. **Medicines you shouldn't take right now, but may take later**: These are medications that you will take again when it is safe for you to do so. Put these in a separate bag away from category #2 medications until you are seen by

your primary care physician.

Speaking of primary care physicians, I want you to call their office after you leave the hospital to do a few more things:

1. **Confirm your appointment.** It should have been set up while you were in the hospital, but if it's not, make sure you get yourself on the books.
2. **Ask what paperwork they want you to bring to the appointment.** Your primary care physician may have access to your hospital records if they have an electronic medical record that is associated with the hospital, but some may not. In that case, they may ask you to bring your discharge paperwork and/or a discharge summary.

Now, when the time comes for you to actually visit your primary care physician, there are three things I want you to bring with you:

1. Your medication reconciliation list from the hospital
2. All your medications, separated into three bags as previously discussed
3. Any paperwork your PCP's office requested and any paperwork you will need your PCP to complete

Your primary care doctor will go over these medications with you and do another medication reconciliation of sorts. They may recommend you start back up on a prior one, start one that was on hold, or stop taking a new one. It's possible that adjustments will be made to your medication routine at that visit or even a little while afterward.

Dietary Prescriptions

After a hospitalization, other adjustments may have been made to your lifestyle beyond just the medicines you are prescribed. Jumping back to your first day home, I want you to focus on your diet (if you've had a change in that department). Head over to your kitchen, take a peek in the fridge, and start coming up with a plan for how you're going to follow the new dietary prescription you've been given. This step may mean getting rid of high-salt foods, limiting your sugar intake, or even changing the texture of the foods you eat.

Oftentimes, this change is a lifelong one, so I want you to give yourself a little grace if this applies to you. Nobody gets diagnosed with diabetes on Tuesday and becomes a perfect eater on Wednesday. It's going to take a lot of trial and error to find something that works for you.

But there's a reason why I call it dietary prescriptions instead of dietary restrictions. You really shouldn't look at your new diet as everything you can't have, but more as what the doctor prescribes to *help support your general health and address specific medical needs.*

Physical Therapies and Equipment

If you are coming home and moving a little more slowly or a little differently than when you went to the hospital, you are likely also coming home with some new equipment to help you move about. You may have crutches, a cane, or a walker to help steady you.

If you are given something, please use it. If you are given a shower chair, please use it; falling in the tub or shower can be disastrous. If you are given a bedside commode or an elevated toilet seat, please use it; I guarantee it will make toileting and caring for yourself easier and safer. All of these pieces of equipment are for your safety and will make life at home easier, faster, and smoother for you. As a note, you should use any new equipment as instructed until you are evaluated and deemed to no longer need it.

The other thing that will help you be safe in your home and get better faster is to participate in any physical therapy (PT) that you are prescribed. Go to the PT appointments even if you don't feel like it, or let the therapist visit you at home even if on that day you wish they would go away.

PT is really extremely beneficial, and its only limitation is the amount of effort that you put into it. Remember, that a body at rest will stay at rest, so get up and be active by participating in PT and doing the exercises prescribed to you. Physical therapy will make you stronger, safer around your home, and able to do all the things you want to do.

Time to Relax

When all of the above is done, try to find the peace you need to recover. Get comfortable and be happy you're home. I also want you to start to think about the ways you're going to stay out of the hospital. Or, if you know that you're going to have to go back to the hospital for something scheduled, start planning for that.

Go back to "Pre-Day One" and start there. Pack your bags. Make sure you have a list of your medications. Grab a new notepad for your questions and notes.

Start over again and take solace in the fact that you are an active participant in your health, are well-prepared for the hospital, and are much better off with the knowledge you have now than you'd be otherwise.

After Discharge

Now that you've reached the end of this book, I hope that this guide has made a difference in your hospitalization. I also hope that you were able to clearly communicate your big and little goals every day you were in the hospital, that there was never a question that went unanswered, and that you or your loved one recover well, wherever you may be.

Now that you or your loved one is in active recovery, remember that the word *active* is in that phrase. Over the next few days, weeks, or even months, you will need to participate in your care so you can get back to your best level of functioning possible.

Please remember to do the following:

- Perform an at-home medication reconciliation
- Follow up with your primary care physician and/or specialists
- Check in with your support system and surround yourself with the people you love

Phew! I promise that's the last bit of direction I'll give you in this book. Hopefully, you or your loved one won't have to go through another hospitalization, but if you do, just go back to "Pre-Day One."

Goodbye for Now

There are certain physicians whom people tend to be happy to see at the hospital because it means something is going to get better. Everybody's happy to walk out of the hospital with a brand-new baby or a new knee that doesn't hurt anymore—both of which are very exciting things.

The sad truth for me is that people are rarely happy to meet a hospitalist.

Meeting a hospitalist means you've probably just been stuck with a bunch of needles and are in a ton of pain. It also means the next four or five more days are going to be spent the exact same way—with you being stuck in bed, poked, and prodded for more tests. Furthermore, there may be conversations about new diagnoses or more invasive treatments that will be needed. Even when a hospitalist's work is done, the patient may still leave the hospital feeling less than their usual self, or perhaps hospice care has been started.

However, since I've been working as a hospitalist, I have seen that it's actually possible for people to enjoy their hospitalization. As a physician leader, I get letters about my colleagues and the great work they do all the time.

So, yes, it's possible to have a good experience in the hospital even with an unexpected hospitalization. I think the things that makes this possible are clear and consistent communication and realistic expectations being set and met by both the patient and the care team. I want more people to have this experience in the hospital because I know it can be done, so I hope this book has brought you closer to that in some shape or form.

That brings me to my final bow! Thank you for taking the time to read this book. It means so much that you've trusted me with the task of giving you this information.

Most importantly, I hope that this book allowed you to be more prepared, calm, and confident in the hospital.

In Memory of Dr. Robert K. McIntyre

We miss you, Bob

www.ingramcontent.com/pod-product-compliance
Lightning Source LLC
LaVergne TN
LVHW041932070526
838199LV00051BA/2786

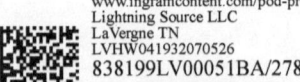